Table of Contents

[Title Page](#)

[Copyright](#)

[Prologue](#)

[Chapter One](#)

[Chapter Two](#)

[Chapter Three](#)

[Chapter Four](#)

[Chapter Five](#)

[Chapter Six](#)

[Chapter Seven](#)

[Chapter Eight](#)

[Chapter Nine](#)

[Chapter Ten](#)

[Chapter Eleven](#)

[Chapter Twelve](#)

[Chapter Thirteen](#)

[Epilogue](#)

[Anything for Love Sneak Peak](#)

[Other Titles By Jena Wade](#)

[About Jena Wade](#)

Crying Out Loud

Millerstown Moments

Book Three

Jena Wade
Lorelei M. Hart

Copyright © 2019 by Jena Wade & Lorelei M. Hart
All rights reserved. This copy is intended for the original purchaser of this e-book ONLY. No part of this e-book may be reproduced, scanned, or distributed in any printed or electronic form without prior written permission from the author. Please do not participate in or encourage piracy of copyrighted materials in violation of the author's rights. Purchase only authorized editions.
Image/art disclaimer: Licensed material is being used for illustrative purposes only. Any person depicted in the licensed material is a model.
Icon made by https://www.freepik.com/ from www.flaticon.com
Published in the United States of America
This e-book is a work of fiction. While reference might be made to actual historical events or existing locations, the names, characters, places and incidents are either the product of the author's imagination or are used fictitiously, and any resemblance to actual persons, living or dead, business establishments, events, or locales is entirely coincidental.
www.thejenawade.com
www.mpregwithhart.com
Warning
This e-book contains sexually explicit scenes and adult language and may be considered offensive to some readers. Jena Wade's e-books are for sale to adults ONLY, as defined by the laws of the country in which you made your purchase. Please store your files wisely, where they cannot be accessed by under-aged readers.

Prologue

Cam

The police department was ahead of us by three runs when I came up to bat. The pitch was perfect, straight down the center, and I managed to hit the ball far into left field. The bases were loaded, of course, and runners made their way around, coming into home. I should have stopped at third and called it good, but my adrenaline was pumping, my heart pounding. When I rounded third, I saw Police Chief Derek Williams standing at home plate, blocking my way, and I was determined to plow right through him and score another run for my team.

I didn't count on the left fielder throwing the ball in. As I thundered down the third base line, I watched as Derek braced for the catch. The ball landed smoothly in his glove just as I plowed right into his middle, knocking him to the ground.

We landed on top of home plate. He was flat on his back, me on top of him. He'd thrown his mask off, my forehead rested against his, our hips touching, our breathing heavy. His mitt was sandwiched between us and I felt the bulge of the ball in his glove. I was out. We had lost. The police department would be the reigning champs for another year and had bragging rights as well. I was too captivated by Derek's eyes to look away.

I was younger than Derek by at least fifteen years, one of the youngest firemen on the crew and the only Omega. Because of that, I had to work harder, be faster, better, stronger than all of them, so that my Omega status didn't get in the way of my accomplishments.

I couldn't let anyone know that I was at the mercy of my body's response to this Alpha. But I was, anytime I came near Derek, and I was near him often, since we both worked for the town. The police station was across the street from the fire station. I interacted with him plenty, and my body responded the same way every time. Hard. Ready. Wanting.

"Out!" the umpire screamed, and the police force went wild.

Derek's eyes turn dark. Arousal or anger? I couldn't tell.

"Are you going to get off me, Omega?"

I gave him a half smile despite the aching in my joints. "I'd like to help you get off, Chief," I said.

After a moment, I did get to my feet and then helped him up. He didn't look at me, just walked away as if I didn't exist, which is generally what he did anyway. Derek never looked in my direction. The man probably didn't even know my name, which was fine. We could keep it that way. But damn, he looked good in a pair of baseball pants. Almost as good as in his uniform.

I made my way back to the fire station dugout. The guys gave me pats on the back. "It was a good hit, Cam. We'll get them next year."

***

The firemen decided we'd meet up at the bar later that evening to commiserate over our loss. Nobody blamed me, thankfully. Although I knew I should have stayed put on third base. We would have tied and gone into extra innings or simply been content with a tie. Either way, it wouldn't have been a loss. But when I'd seen Chief Williams standing there like my own personal target, I couldn't resist.

Many of the firemen were trying to pick up Omegas; a few of them were succeeding. Then there was me, the lonely single Omega at the bar. None of the Alphas in the room were looking my way. As far as Omegas went, I wasn't bad looking, but I most certainly wasn't the dainty little thing many Alphas preferred. I towered over most people at six-foot-four, and my bulky muscles made me more than a little intimidating.

I signaled the bartender for my tab because I might as well go home. There was no point in staying out any later. But then he walked in. The air shifted the moment the door opened and Derek stepped inside. I felt it, though no one around me seemed to notice.

He sat on the barstool beside me and motioned for a drink. The bartender set his beer in front of him at the same time he gave me my tab. I caught a glimpse of Derek. Dark circles marred his eyes. I knew that look, I'd worn it a time or two myself. In our line of work, tough days came with the job, and some days were worse than others. Based on the look on Derek's face, his day after the game had been awful.

"Everything all right?" I asked.

He scrubbed his hands over his face. "No."

"You want to talk about it?".

He looked at me, his eyes hungry with need. "Not particularly."

I don't know what sparked inside me at that moment, but I got an influx of confidence. I wanted to take his mind off his troubles, for a little while. "You want to get out of here then?"

"Yeah," he said. "I do." He threw a twenty down, which would most certainly cover the beer he had bought but hadn't even taken a drink of. I tossed in another twenty to cover my tab.

I lived right inside of town, so I walked everywhere I went, including the bar that night. So, when I saw his squad car outside with *Chief of Police* written on the side of it, I got in.

"What happened?" I asked.

He shook his head. "Drug overdose."

"In Millerstown? Damn."

"Yeah," he said. "That shit's everywhere. The guy's alive, though. Don't know how, but he is."

"Lucky fucker," I said.

"Maybe, maybe not." Derek shook his head. "His kid's safe now, that's all that matters."

"Fuck, he's got a kid? Anyone I know?"

"Can we change the subject? I don't want to talk about it."

"All right." I knew what the score was. Derek needed something to distract him from his job. I needed to experience Derek at least once. Then, maybe I could get him out of my mind permanently. I doubted it, but it was worth a shot. It was nearly midnight when we got to his house.

"You hungry?" he asked.

I shook my head. "I didn't come over here for food."

"No," he said. "You didn't."

Derek closed the space between us, his eyes almost level with mine. He placed his hand on the back of my neck and pulled me in for a hard kiss. I melted against him. His lips crushed against mine, but I didn't care because I had Derrick Williams in my arms, and soon he'd have me in his bed.

I barely registered that he was unbuckling my pants and tugging at my shirt until our kiss broke and he pulled my shirt over my head then whipped my pants down. I stepped out of them, and he tossed them into a corner.

His clothes disappeared as well, and we made our way toward the bedroom. I kissed and touched and explored as much as I could as we walked. This would be a night I wouldn't soon forget. I only hoped that it wouldn't be our only night together, though I doubted Derek would come back for more.

He seemed determined to get this over with quickly. I wondered if he even knew my name. I could pretend he did.

I lay on my back on the bed. He motioned for me to flip over, and I complied. Pretending I was someone else? *Maybe.* I'd allow it, though.

Derek nudged my legs apart, and I pulled my knees underneath me. He rummaged through the nightstand and pulled some items out. I couldn't see what they were.

"Condom?" I asked.

"Yeah."

He was behind me again, his fingers at my opening, gently caressing until my body welcomed him in. My channel accommodated his fingers easily, my Omega nature ready for an Alpha to lay their claim.

His fingers were soon replaced with his cock. He pushed into me slowly. I moaned and pushed back against him, wanting all of him at once.

"Fuck me, Derek,"

He chuckled. "Your wish is my command." He slammed into me, and I fisted my hands in the blanket to hold onto something. I cried out in pleasure as his cock filled me to the brim.

His hands held my hips in place. My dick ached with need, and my hand went to it, pumping to the same rhythm my Alpha maintained.

I'd thought about being this way for so long I was halfway to the edge before we'd even started, so I wasn't surprised when I came. I groaned and arched into Derek.

His fingers tightened on my hips, likely leaving marks, as he roared his release soon after.

My knees gave out, and Derek collapsed on top of me. A big guy like me could hold his weight just fine, and it felt nice to be cocooned by him, held tight and safe. But then he was gone.

The cool air hit my back, and I knew the fun was over.

He disappeared into the bathroom, and I grabbed a tissue from the nightstand to clean myself up. He came back a moment later and stripped the bed of the blanket.

"Is a sheet fine, or do you need a blanket to sleep with?"

I looked at him in surprise. "I assumed I was going home."

"Fuck, Cam, I'm not that much of an asshole that I'm going to make you walk home after that. Stay the night."

So, he did know my name. "Okay."

I climbed back on to the bed, and Derek joined me.

***

I woke up to the smell of coffee, which usually meant it was going to be a good morning. The only time I woke up to coffee being ready was when I was at the station. Only, this bed was thirty times more comfortable than the station bunks.

The night came back to me in a rush. I was at Derek's house, in Derek's bed. I sat up and found my clothes folded neatly at the edge of the bed. I pulled them on and exited the room.

Derek was at the table. He had his laptop out and stared intently at the screen.

"Good morning," I said.

He grunted. "It's closer to afternoon than morning."

"What?"

He turned to look at me then, glasses perched on his nose. "You slept most of the morning. I checked the schedule, and you're not on shift until tomorrow, so I figured I'd let you sleep."

"Thanks," I said.

He closed his laptop and stood. "Listen, last night was fun."

I winced. It was unlikely that he was going to follow that up with "We should do it again sometime."

"Yeah, but it can't ever happen again, right? You're just not into me? Or is it that you can't get into a relationship right now? Or, are you going to be completely honest and say an Omega of my size is not appealing enough to fuck twice? Pick one. I've heard them all."

He narrowed his eyes. "It's just not a good idea. You're young, way younger than me. And we're technically colleagues."

I nodded. "Well, I'll see you around then." No use in arguing and laying my heart out there like a fool.

I opened the door and ran straight into Turner Jefferies, one of Derek's officers. Fuck. We did not need that. I tried to come up with an excuse as to why I'd be here in my clothes from yesterday, but I couldn't.

Fuck it. Derek can come up with an excuse.

I nodded to Jeffries and walked out the door.

Chapter One

Cam

I checked the last of the oxygen tanks for the third time. Better safe than sorry, of course, but rather than worrying about safety, I was avoiding the conversation happening thirty feet away from me in the open garage area of the fire station. Why they couldn't just take the conversation to the office?

Fire Chief Barry Hughes stood with Philip Miller, a close friend of mine and fellow firefighter, and newly appointed Deputy Police Chief Turner Jeffries, and finally, Derek Williams, police chief extraordinaire. Normally, I would have no problem taking part in the conversation. After all, I was a fireman, he was a police chief, and our paths had crossed a time or two. It was a small town, and I'd easily hid the crush I'd been harboring for years. Way too many years.

But after what had happened four months ago, he and I hadn't as much so looked at each other, which was getting harder and harder. As the newly elected mayor, Harrison Bowman had more and more ideas on how to unify and better the town after the scandal had ripped through it. He'd served as interim mayor for a few months after Ian Miller's arrest, and a few months ago he'd won the special election. Part of his plan was to have the firemen and policemen work closer together.

I wasn't going to put myself in Derek's path if I didn't have to. The night the two of us had spent together had been amazing, but there would not be a repeat.

A shadow crossed my line of sight, and I looked up to find Philip standing there.

"You have to go home," he said.

I stood and looked at him. "Why?" I glanced at the clock on the wall. My shift wasn't over yet.

"You're maxed out on hours. Actually, you maxed out on hours yesterday, but I didn't realize it until this morning."

"What?" I said. "Let me see that." I looked over the time sheet that he had printed out. "No, when I was here on Tuesday I wasn't working."

Philip shook his head. "You went out on a run with us, right?"

"Well, yeah, but it wasn't a fire. I mean, I didn't do anything."

"Doesn't matter. It's recorded on the timesheet. You were working. Go home. Learn a little something about work/life balance."

I snorted. That was hard to achieve, since I didn't have much of a personal life. My work was my life. I glanced around the area quickly, but I knew Derek was no longer there. I'd feel him if he was still in the room.

"Looking for a certain police chief?" Philip asked.

"What? No," I said. "Why would you think that? Did Turner tell you?"

Philip cocked his head to the side, and a slow smile spread across his face. "No," he said slowly. "What does Turner know?"

Fuck. I walked right into that. Four months of keeping it to myself, and I slipped up. *Fuck.*

"Never mind. Do you have the schedule for next month yet?"

Philip shook his head. "Haven't had time to get it done with all the stuff the new mayor wants. Which is great, don't get me wrong. I swear I'm up to my ears in paperwork, though."

"I can help," I said. Anything to keep me busy, to keep me thinking about anything besides Derek.

Philip narrowed his eyes at me and remained quiet. "I'll think about it," he said. "I could use the help, and I think you just might be the man for the job. Let me talk it over with Barry."

"Thanks." I grabbed my jacket and headed out the door. I didn't really need a jacket for the late fall morning, but it wouldn't be long before the temperatures dropped to nearly freezing levels.

***

I went back to the duplex I called my home. I had been renting it for five years now, since the owner had retired and move to Florida. I'm not even sure why he held on to the property anymore, but he was easy to work with, and the rent was cheap so I couldn't complain. I took care of most of my own repairs, and he knocked a few bucks off the rent when I did that sort of thing.

Over the years, I'd gotten different neighbors. Nobody stayed for very long. Currently, I had an Alpha and Omega couple living next door. They kept to themselves. I had no idea what they did for work because they were home most of the time. At least I think they were home most of the time. I was hardly ever there, so how was I supposed to know? We'd waved to each other a few times, but mostly we didn't interact, which was what I preferred.

I sat on my couch with my feet up, flipping through channels. When I determined there was nothing on, I shut off the TV and grabbed my tablet off the table and settled in.

I was quite engrossed in the last chapter of my book when the shouting started. It began with a slammed door and some yelling back and forth about somebody not picking up the right products. I shook my head. Couples arguing over grocery lists. Must be a match made in heaven. Then the shouts got louder, and I couldn't help but listen in.

"You didn't get the right stuff for Marcus."

"Fuck Marcus," the other said. "I can sell this shit on my own. I don't need him."

"You're such a fucking idiot, Nick. We can't market this on our own. We're going to end up in jail. I'm calling Marcus."

"You fucking call Marcus, and I swear I will kill you right now." The tone of his voice told me he wasn't messing around. Whatever they were into was serious.

"Oh shit," I said and bolted up right. This wasn't a typical argument that couples had, at least I hoped not. But what did I know? I'd never been in a relationship.

"Fine. We'll do what you want. But this wasn't in the agreement."

There was a loud noise like a body slammed against a wall. and the picture frame on my side shook.

"I make the rules now. Do you understand? Don't you cross me. We've got a lot of product to push, and if we get this all sold, we can leave this town and start up someplace fresh. With our own damn money."

"All right, fine. Whatever you say."

"That's a good Omega."

"Fuck," I said. I picked up my cell phone and dialed, going to the far corner of my house so that the other inhabitants didn't hear.

"Millerstown PD. How can I help you?"

I'd recognize that voice anywhere, though it surprised me Derek was handling dispatch. I was at a loss for words. How does one even report a crime?

"Hello? Is anyone there? I swear to God, if this is teenagers crank calling again, I'm going to lose my shit."

"It's not," I said. "It's me. Cam."

"Oh. Hi."

"Hi," I said.

"Were you calling for anything in particular? Or…"

I shook my head, trying to organize my thoughts. "Oh, yeah. My neighbors…."

"You got a noise complaint?" Derek asked.

"No. Not that. I, ugh, I think they're drug dealers" I realized just how insane that sounded.

"You think what?" Derek said.

"I overheard a conversation, and one of the guys threatened to kill the other, and he mentioned something about a product, and Marcus and…" I wasn't making any sense. "Listen, Chief, I'm not crazy."

"All right. I believe you," he said. "Tell me what happened."

I recounted the conversation as I remembered it, and he remained silent for a minute.

"Okay," he said. "I'm going to come over with Jeffries and have them taken in for questioning."

"Already?"

"Yeah," he replied. "I've got an anonymous tip that says there's drugs in the house. Plus, I'm sure you wouldn't mind filing a noise complaint."

"Sure."

"Sit tight, and don't do anything stupid. We'll be there in a few minutes."

"Okay." I put the phone down. What in the hell did one do with oneself when the police were coming over to raid the neighbors?

Chapter Two

Derek

This was Millerstown. And sure, there were drugs. More and more by the day — or so it felt, but to hear they were so close that a friend had to call in their neighbor? That had me sideswiped.

Not that Cam was a friend. Not really. He was a one-night stand — a person I shared a good time with. That was all. So what if it was the best sex of my life? So what if I couldn't stop thinking about him? So what if I whacked off to the memory of him naked, wrapped so tightly around my cock? So what if he was too young for me?

"Derek, ready?" Jeffries' hand settled on my shoulder.

"Yeah, ready. Just trying to figure out if we need backup," I lied.

"It is probably pot. If it was really bad shit, they'd be quieter about it. People think because pot is legal in some places and most people seem to be cool with it, that they can just talk about it willy nilly." He shrugged.

He was probably right, and I pushed down the nagging feeling in my gut as we climbed in the car and drove to the duplex where Cam lived. It was not the most high-end place in town, but it was nice enough.

"How are we going to play this? If we go in with the typical noise complaint, they will know it was Cam." He knew about my night with Cam, and to the best of my knowledge, he was the only one who did. He'd never said anything about it, though. Turner Jeffries was a man who could keep a secret, being a former FBI agent and all.

"Knock on the door and say hello," I said.

He nodded.

My heart rate kicked up a notch, like it always did when I was near Cam. Try as I might, he was never out of my thoughts.

Puke. Stepping in dog poop. Sweet pickles in custard. I was thinking of any and all things to control my libido. Turned out I didn't need to. Jeffries took care of it all by himself.

"Have you and Cam hooked up since the softball game?" Of course he'd ask that right now. Probably a ton of people had seen us leave together, but they'd all had the decency not to mention it. And only Turner *knew* that we'd spent the night together.

"No." Unfortunately.

We turned the corner. Only three blocks to go. Jeffries pointed to the siren control, but I shook my head. That was the last thing we needed. Nope. In and out. Done.

"Ah ha, so you did sleep with him." He pretended he'd just pieced it together. "He's a little young for an old man like you, don't you think?"

"He is not even close to jailbait, asshole." We pulled up to the townhouse, effectively ending the conversation. Not that he wasn't going to bring it up again. Now that he knew it got a rise out of me it, would become his boredom relief until he found something else.

"Just knocking for a *safety* check?" Jeffries suggested.

"Yeah, sure." The last thing we wanted to do was to go in, guns drawn like they did on so many stupid television shows. Not only would guns being drawn mean a shit-ton of paperwork, but they also agitated people. If Cam had called it correctly, they at the very least were under the influence of something, and at the very worst selling some of their stash. Or at least that was my assumption.

How beyond wrong I was.

Within five minutes of knocking on the door, we had our guns drawn, an Omega cornered in the house, and an Alpha racing out the back entrance.

Turner took off on foot after him, while I called for backup. It turned out, we not only had discovered some druggies, we had found a fucking meth lab—in Millerstown.

As backup from our department arrived, the Omega barricaded in the kitchen panicked. Jeffries had radioed the police department in Rochdale, the nearest town to Millerstown. They'd arrived quickly as well.

I stood outside the closed door, gun drawn but pointed toward the ground. "Come out with your hands up."

"Fuck you!"

They never could make it easy.

We were lucky Rochdale and Millerstown had an agreement to help in situations like this. I had no idea what I'd have done otherwise. As it was, all I wanted to do was get Cam out of the other side of the duplex and away from this mess.

There was a sizzling sound and a resounding pop from behind the door. A terrible feeling settled in the pit of my stomach.

"Evacuate! Evacuate!"

So much for protocol, the man was going to take us all out with whatever the hell he was doing in there. An ammonia smell permeated the air.

"I'm getting Cam out. We need to clear the area," I shouted to my detectives on the scene.

I ran to Cam's door, and was banging on it when all hell broke loose, the entire structure shaking. I fell to the ground.

Not. Good.

I managed to get back up and broke down Cam's door. Thank fuck whoever built the place had used the cheapest materials ever because the thing popped open with ease.

"Cam!" I called into the open space.

"Look down." He had an almost teasing lilt to his voice, and when I looked down, I saw why. He was on the floor in the middle of the room, his leg at a very odd angle. The wall shared with the other portion of the duplex had bowed at the center, and the creaking of wood echoed throughout the room.

"Shit." I ran over and knelt. "What happened?"

"I fell, and I can't get up," he teased, although there was nothing funny about it.

Voices called from outside as fire sirens blared. Smoke filtered through the cracks in the wall.

"We need to get you out of here." I scooped him up and walked him straight out to a waiting ambulance.

It wasn't until he was tucked away inside, headed to the hospital, that I focused again on the scene around me. The Omega in the kitchen had caused an explosion, deciding that he'd take everyone down with him over going to jail.

More and more people arrived on the scene. In all my years on the force, we hadn't had to deal with an actual meth lab. We'd had all the training, but this was our first meth lab bust. Thank God for Jeffries and his expertise from being in the FBI. When the state showed up to take over, relief started to settle in—and so did my cough.

"Go get yourself checked out, Derek," Jeffries insisted. "That is an order."

"You are not the boss of me." I had planned to keep the banter going, but the cough took over. When it finally stopped, I agreed to get checked out. There was nothing more I could do where I was. The fire was under control, and the scene was swarming with more police and troopers than we'd ever needed before.

One of my officers drove me to the hospital and it turned out, I was fine, just irritated by something or other—I hadn't really been paying attention. Whose idea was it to explain what was going on while giving a breathing treatment?

The ER was a fairly open space, which was horrible for patient privacy but meant I was able to get a glimpse of Cam twice in the time I was there. I watched him being wheeled to X-ray and back, or at least that was what the tech pushing his bed said because yeah, I was a creeper and focused more on the Omega than on my own health.

I hopped out of bed after everyone had vacated my little curtain-divided room, on a mission to see if Cam was all right—as all right as he could be given his leg injury.

I found him with ease, stopping dead in my tracks as I heard the doctor say, "The good news is the baby is fine."

"What baby?" Cam asked, voice shaking.

That was my question, too.

Chapter Three

Cam

"This is ridiculous. I don't need to be here. The doctor was mistaken. There is no way I'm pregnant," I said for the thousandth time.

Derek sat in a chair in the corner of the room they'd moved us to after the doctor's little announcement. He scrubbed his face with his hands. The poor guy looked worn out, like he could use a nap. It been a rough day for the police force. "For the last time, you do need to be here. If you think you can go home, you're welcome to walk out of here."

"Fine." I crossed my arms over my chest. "I need to be here so we can figure out what the fuck is going on with my leg. You don't need to be here. Don't you want to be at the scene?"

"I trust my officers to handle it. Especially Turner. Hell, I couldn't pick a better guy to handle this situation. Fucking drugs in Millerstown."

"Yeah," I said. "Fucking drugs right next door."

"You'd never heard anything between those guys before?"

I shook my head. Concentrating on something else other than the pain helped. "No. I'm not home all that much, and they seem to be home all the time. At least, I've never seen their car gone. They were quiet until today. Was it meth?"

He nodded. Probably couldn't tell me more due to the open investigation and all that. "How did you manage to fall anyway?"

Ugh. I really didn't want to admit that one to him. "I was listening with my ear against the wall. I was smart enough to step away when things started getting crazy, but the explosion startled me, and I tripped."

Thankfully, Derek didn't laugh.

The nurse had come in every thirty minutes to take in my blood pressure, heart rate, and, at one point had drawn some blood to run tests. I'd just gotten back from X-ray when the doctor had dropped the news. He was wrong, but it had still shaken me.

I couldn't be pregnant. There was no way.

The curtain was pushed aside, and the doctor came in. "Good morning," he said and then checked his watch. "Nope. Afternoon." He laughed, like it was a funny joke. I wasn't feeling particularly comedic, but I gave him a smile. "All right," he said. "Got some good news. The leg is broken."

"That's good news?" I said.

"Well, you're going to be able to keep it." He laughed again. All right, now the humor was getting annoying.

"Give it to us straight, Doc, please?" Derek said. "We don't have a lot of time. He'd like to get home."

"Well, that's great," the doctor said. "But I'd really like to keep him for an ultrasound. So, we can get look at the baby to make sure that little peanut is all right."

"Doc, I appreciate your bedside manner with the humor and all that, but I'm not pregnant. You've got the wrong room or the tests are throwing false positives or something."

The doctor narrowed his eyes, looked at his chart, and flipped the page. "You're Cameron O'Neill, and you just came from the meth house bust, right?"

"Yeah," I said.

"Well, we tested your blood just in case we needed to operate, which we don't. So, that's a good point, and you're pregnant. You didn't know?"

I laughed. "No, I didn't know because I'm not pregnant." I looked over at Derek, whose eyes were wide.

"Is it possible, Cam?"

"No," I said. "I'm not. I mean. No, I can't be. I haven't been with anyone..."

"Since four months ago?" Derek said.

My cheeks burned. "Yeah, and we would have known before then. I mean, I'd be showing." I patted my stomach, which was slightly more rounded than it had been in the past. But I'd also been eating out a lot. I regularly had whole pizzas for dinner, because why the fuck would I cook for myself when it was just me? And when I was visiting the guys while I was off shift, I usually brought them a dozen donuts, which ended up being just ten donuts. Since I took my fair share. "I can't be." I said. "The tests are wrong."

"No, the tests are pretty conclusive. But if you'd like we can draw some more blood and run them again or just have you take an over-the-counter test," the doctor suggested.

"Whatever gets us the results quicker and me out of here."

"All right. I'll put the order in, and in the meantime, we're going to have you fitted in a cast. I'll have the orthopedic doctor talk to you about your limitations and the physical therapy."

I pinched the bridge of my nose and leaned back on the bed. The uncomfortable bed. Fuck. I wouldn't be able to work. I couldn't fight fires with a broken leg, and my house was a crime scene.

"You can really go home now," I said to Derek. "This is going to take forever. Discharge paperwork always does—"

"Cam," Derek said. His voice low and serious.

I opened an eye and looked at him. "What?"

"Are you pregnant?"

"No, Jesus," I said. "I'd know by now."

"You haven't been with anyone?"

"No." I shook my head and shrugged like it was no big deal. Like I wasn't pining for him each and every day. "I mean, I've just been busy with work. So I haven't gone out much. There's not a lot of single Alphas around here, you know?" Actually, there were plenty of single people, Alphas and Omegas, in Millerstown, but none of them were Derek.

"Uh huh." He nodded. "I haven't been with anyone either." He sat there quietly, hands folded in his lap, and I went back to resting.

A nurse came in, and Derek gave us some privacy while she helped me do my business so we could run this test. Then she took another vial of blood for good measure. "We'll have the results in just a couple of minutes from the test. The blood work will come back later, though."

"All right," I said. "It'll be negative." It had to be negative.

Two minutes later, she was back in the room. "Congratulations," she said and smiled at both of us.

"See," I said. "I told you there's nothing to worry about."

"You're pregnant, and I understand you're about four months along?" she continued.

"What?" I said. "I thought that the test was negative."

"No," she said. "Positive. It's pretty rare to get a false positive on these also. They make them pretty good these days."

"Oh, fuck." I looked at Derek. I tried to come up with something to say, but my mind blanked. He stared back at me, horror on his face.

"Oh fuck," he said.

***

Derek and I didn't get a chance to talk because the orthopedic doctor came in then. He explained about my break, gave me a few printouts and resources about how to take care of my leg, explaining what I could and couldn't do.

I barely listened. It was hard to focus.

He put my leg in a temporary cast, telling me that in a week or so I'd get a boot I could walk in. But for the first week to ten days, he wanted me to stay off the leg as much as possible, meaning I was to be planted on a couch with my foot elevated for 95 percent of the time.

I had no idea how'd I manage that.

"Can I go home now?" I asked him as he was finishing up the cast.

"Nope. As I understand it, they want you to get an ultrasound done."

Oh Christ. I was going to be here forever.

I nodded my thanks as he left.

Once Derek and I were alone again, I looked at him. His face was still frozen in surprise.

"So, prior to being with me four months ago…?" He started.

I sighed. "Do you want me to lie to you and tell you that there have been plenty of other Alphas so you can be off the hook? If you want that, just tell me right now, and I'll set you free of whatever responsibilities you think you might have."

"Just tell me the truth, Cam."

"I think you already know the truth, Derek. You're the only Alpha I've been with in six or seven months. I can't remember exactly."

He nodded. "That's what I suspected."

"Look," I said. "I'm still a little out of it. It's been a hell of a day. We don't have to discuss anything today. If you'd like, you can go home or go back to the crime scene and do whatever needs doing—"

"Just stop, Cam. All right? I'm not going anywhere. I'm not overwhelmed by this whole day. Yeah, it's been a crazy one, but I'm not a child. I can manage it. And have you thought about the fact you don't have any place to go?"

"I—" I was about to protest and tell him I could go plenty of places, but he was right. I didn't have any family nearby. My closest friend, Alex, was out of town going to school at the moment, and he didn't keep an apartment in Millerstown when he was in school. I was, essentially, fucked. "I can ask Philip."

"No. They've got a full house with a daycare, and Ollie is going to pop any day now," Derek said. "You're coming home with me."

"Like hell I am," I insisted. "I think I can decide where I'm going to stay."

"Oh, really? And who's going to come pick you up to take you there?"

"So, this is what you're going to do now? Hold me hostage?"

"No, but I'm asking you to be realistic. Just think about it. I'm offering you a place to stay while you recover. It's not like you can go back to your house."

I closed my eyes. I felt a headache creeping on and just wanted to fall asleep and forget this day happened. Maybe it was all just a dream. "Fine," I said. "I'll come back to your house. But I still don't expect anything from you. Just because this is your baby doesn't mean I'm going to demand you man up or whatever the fuck and become my Alpha. I can take care of myself."

Derek remained quiet. Before he could say anything, the doctor came back into the room with a large machine on wheels.

"Time for the ultrasound," he said.

My breath caught as the doctor put the ultrasound wand to my still mostly flat stomach. The picture came onto the screen. Derek came close to my side, his hand resting on my shoulder as he watched the screen as well. His face held awe. This was our baby. A life that we created together...however unplanned it may be, it was ours.

"Is the baby okay?" I asked.

"He appears to be," the doctor said. "You're measuring a little smaller than the four months you say it's been, but that's all right. The one thing I am concerned about though is the baby's heart rate. It's not quite in the range we'd like to see. I think it would be best if we had you stay overnight for observation."

"I can do that." I swallowed thickly and nodded. "I don't have any place to go anyway."

"You're coming home with me. You're welcome to stay as long as you need to," Derek said.

"I know."

"I'll get the house ready for you. Is there anything he needs, Doctor? For the baby or whatever?"

"Prenatal vitamins," the doctor said. "We can write you a prescription, or they sell them over the counter. You'll want to grab the Omega kind."

Derek nodded, taking his job as expectant father very seriously.

The doctor put the wand away and cleaned my stomach. He handed me a printed picture of our baby. I could just make out its head and feet in the grainy image.

"You'll want to make an appointment with your Omega specialist as well."

I nodded. "I'll do that."

"Since you're this far along, you should be able to tell the gender pretty soon."

I grinned, turning toward Derek. He smiled, his eyes fixed on the pictured I held in my hand.

Chapter Four

Derek

Leaving the hospital was one of the hardest things I'd ever had to do. Knowing that his child—our child—was potentially less than perfect scared the crap out of me. Nowhere in my mind had I been thinking of starting a family right now, not without an Omega and then—boom.

The one Omega I wanted but been too chickenshit to pursue was carrying my baby, and it was time to man up.

My guestroom had morphed into a storage room over the years, and I had plenty to keep me occupied while I waited for Cam to be discharged in the morning. Or, at least, that was my plan. The doctors and our child might have different ideas.

I lugged box after box out of the guestroom and into the basement. Where I really wanted Cam was in my bed—with me. The feelings I'd been squashing came back full throttle.

Once the boxes were gone and the room vacuumed, I felt a lot better. I stripped the bed, washing the sheets so they would be nice and fresh for Cam. Domestic god I was not, but if getting his sheets clothesline fresh made me the Alpha he needed, I was all for it. I even grabbed the quilt my grandmother made me off my bed for him to use. She had told me it was stitched with love and was like a hug. Cam definitely deserved a hug.

And for his place not to have been in an explosion, and for his leg to be whole, and to not feel like he was going through this pregnancy alone. I could at least help him with that bit.

I stiffened my left knee and tried to walk from my front door to his room, getting things that might impede his ability to cross the distance out of the way. Then I did the same from his bedroom, which I became painfully aware was only a few steps from my own, to the bathroom, my very handicap-unfriendly bathroom.

A quick Internet search had me one-clicking a shower bench, a hand bar for the shower, and a special bag to cover his cast while bathing. The thing looked more like plastic wrap than anything legit, but if it held the slightest potential for making his day easier, I was buying it.

From there I meandered into the kitchen. The refrigerator was full of condiments, leftover takeout, and a gallon of milk of questionable age. I wrote a list of things I thought he might want to have on hand, from easy-to-heat-up meals to fresh fruit and everything in between. Was I going overboard? Heck yeah I was, but it was a compulsion by that point in the morning, for it was almost dawn by the time the knock came at my back door.

"Turner." I held the door open for him to come in. I probably should've gone back to the station to find out what had fully gone down, but I'd been distracted. "Sorry, I—"

"You were in a fucking explosion and rescued the Omega you're sweet on. That was enough for your evening. It wasn't as if the paperwork couldn't wait. I just thought you would want to be brought up to speed."

I grabbed a bottle of warm soda off the counter and handed it to him with a shrug.

He liked to razz me for liking my soda warm, yet he always accepted it when offered one.

"What's the word? I heard whispers at the hospital that it was really bad." Or at least that was what I'd assumed when the nurses were gossiping about a new intake down below, their not so secret code word for the morgue.

"The guy who triggered the explosion, Drew Burns, died at the scene. The Alpha who took off on foot got away. I tracked him to a spot where there were tire tracks. He must've had a getaway vehicle ready in case they needed to run." The look in his eyes told me everything. Nick got away.

My Alpha tendencies went on high alert. Nick was a drug dealer—meth at that—so the chances were spectacular that he was going to run, find more meth heads, and then not look back.

Except...

If the Omega who'd died was *his* Omega, Nick wasn't going to let that one go. He'd want revenge. Cam was in danger. No. Just no. *Protect.*

"You have no idea where he is?"

"None." He reached over and, as if thinking better of it, took his hand back. He, too, was being pushed by his Alpha side. We were in freaking Millerstown. Things like this didn't happen here—except when they did. Turner knew that better than anyone, considering what he and his Omega had gone through just months ago. "Between the explosion, Cam getting hurt, and the confusion, he drove off. We aren't even a hundred percent sure who he is, although Cam said it was Nick Graham."

"Did you talk to him at the hospital?" I didn't even try to mask my anger. "He needs to rest."

"He told us at the scene."

Relief set in. It was bad enough Cam had things connected to his body and the noises of the hospital surrounding him. The last thing he needed was the stress of a police interrogation.

"Did you pay any attention at all?" Turner asked.

"I was a little preoccupied." Understatement of the century.

"With your Omega."

"Not my Omega." I was such a fucking liar.

"But you want him to be." He crossed his arms. Smug bastard. Ever since he'd found his Omega after years of being separated, he'd been all about everyone finding their bliss. Of course he did it dressed in smirk.

"He's pregnant." It slipped out before I could reel it in.

"Oh fuck." Why was he upset? It wasn't his soldiers that went overboard. Then again, his Omega, Kayden, was expecting. "I'm sorry, man. I wouldn't have teased you had I known he was taken."

Oh.

"With my baby," I corrected getting up and grabbing a soda, guzzling it down to buy us a few moments of silence so I could compose myself.

Saying it out loud made it so real.

"He hid his pregnancy from you?"

I understood the shock on his face, given his history.

"That fucking sucks." But not enough not to punch his arm hard enough to sting.

"Owww!"

I growled. "He didn't even know. He was just as shocked by the news as I was. I think possibly more so."

"All right, we're going to have to come back to all of this." Crap, there was more to the bust if he was willing—no insistent on—putting a pregnancy conversation on hold.

"But?"

"His place is a total loss." Which I had assumed, but hearing it spoken solidified things. "Even if the meth contamination could be cleaned to a level of safety, which is highly improbable, the foundation is shot. How Cam managed to get out of there with only a broken leg was a miracle. Wait—if he only has a broken leg, why is he still there?"

And back to the baby it was.

"The baby is measuring small, and the heartbeat was not what they wanted." He would be okay, though. His father was Cam and that made him tough as nails. I'd never known an Omega as strong and capable as Cam.

Not that I'd be upset if the baby was a girl. No, I just wanted the baby—our baby—strong and healthy. I wanted this baby like nothing I'd ever experienced before, which was both exhilarating and terrifying simultaneously.

"Well fuck. Here I am babbling about work. and you need to be with your Omega."

"Not my Omega." *Yet.* "And he needs me here, getting the house ready for when he's discharged."

"And he's okay with this?" His smirk was back.

"I'm not sure he was in his right mind when he agreed." Not that I planned to give him a choice. Not with what I'd just learned. I needed to keep him safe—them safe. "There was no way he was going back to that house, though—none. Especially not while carrying a baby. "Do you think any of his things are salvageable?"

"Doubtful, but some of his buddies were trying to see what they could grab. They said he was going to want his tablet and, of course, some clothes."

Note to self: Look up how to best wash said clothing in case it was contaminated in the explosion.

"He isn't safe with Graham on the loose." Hard. Truth.

"I was just thinking that. I had an idea."

We spent the next few hours hashing out a plan to create a task force. Of course, we would need to bring the mayor in on it, since technically it wouldn't be authorized. Turner was in his element. I could easily see what an asset he'd been to the FBI. Millerstown was lucky to have him.

My Omega was lucky to have him.

Because fuck it. He was mine. Now to figure out a way for him to want me to be his.

Chapter Five

Cam

Derek helped me out of the car and down the sidewalk to his front door. I'd only been to his house the one time and hadn't paid close attention to it. It was a modern ranch-style home, with gray siding and dark-green shutters. The front porch looked nice and cozy, with a swing that overlooked the street.

His landscaping was nice, too, though everything was drying up since the season was almost complete, now that fall was in full swing. In the summer, the plants would be full of color. He didn't strike me as the gardener type, but what did I really know about Derek? Besides the fact that he was the police chief, and that I was incredibly attracted to him, had been since the first moment I'd laid eyes on him.

He held my arm as I limped up the steps not putting any weight on my foot. I used my crutches to lift myself up the stairs. I didn't want to say anything, but the leg throbbed horribly now that I had been upright for a little while.

"We'll get you inside and settled on the couch."

"I'm fine," I said.

"Please. You don't have to pull the tough-guy routine. Your forehead is soaked with sweat."

Yeah, I could definitely feel that.

He got me inside, and I plopped down on the couch, put my foot up on the pillows piled there. Immediately, the throbbing subsided. I inhaled deeply, trying to catch my breath. "Damn. I thought I was in better shape."

"You are," he said. "This is just brand new territory for you. Haven't you ever broken a bone before?"

I shook my head. "Sprained my wrist once when I was a kid, but other than that, I can't say I have."

"I broke my ankle two weeks into the academy. It was a lot of fun, trust me."

"Damn," I said again. "How did you end up passing?"

"Extreme determination. They had to make a few special cases for me, but I managed."

I filed the information away to ask about another day. Derek, I was learning, did not like to talk about himself. Was it just me, or was he like that with everyone?

"Do you need anything? Something to drink? Eat?"

I shook my head.

"Here." He handed me a bottle of water from a collection on an end table nearby. "There's a table I put together for you." He moved the table from where it sat, to right next to me on the couch, on it lay my tablet, two extra battery packs that I assumed were fully charged, a stack of paperbacks I had been reading at home, and a basket full of snacks. Surprisingly enough, they were a lot of my favorites.

"Jesus," I said. "You didn't have to go to all this trouble."

"Well, I wanted you to be comfortable and well taken care of."

I didn't want to admit it, but that made the Omega side of me purr like a damn kitten. My Alpha taking care of me.

He's not yours. I reminded myself, but in the back of my mind, where I let all the ideas that never would come to fruition hide, I wanted him to be.

"Thank you," I said. "I really appreciate it. I'm sorry you've been caught up in this whole mess."

Derek sat down in the recliner next to the couch. "Now, when you say this whole mess, do you mean taking care of you and your broken leg? Or you and the baby?"

"Either? Both? I don't know," I said. "I'm sure this isn't what you signed up for."

Derek shrugged. "Might not be, but here we are," he said. "I'm not going to leave you high and dry and expect you to take care of a child on your own."

I nodded. "I appreciate that. I… I'm keeping the baby," I said.

He raised a brow. "I didn't realize you were thinking of not keeping it."

"I wasn't." I shook my head. "I would never. I just wanted to be clear about that. I'm keeping the baby. It's mine. And yours. If you want, we can work out some sort of situation. Custody, support, and all that." I ran a hand through my hair. Thankfully the nurse had given me a sponge bath of sorts, but damn I would kill for an actual hot shower. "I'm not sure how it's going to work being that I am a firefighter. The three on, two off schedule doesn't seem overly conducive to the single-parent life, but I'll make it work. Somehow," I said. Though I hadn't even begun to think about how that could possibly work.

It had to.

He nodded. "We'll make it work," he said. "This might have been an accident, but we'll get through it together."

"Thank you," I said.

We stared at each other for a moment. Lost in each other's eyes, drowning in possibilities of the future. Us, with a child, together.

The moment was broken though, when a ball of fur leapt into the air and landed on my chest with a thud. "Oomph." I jump forward, jostling my leg.

"Dammit, Cat." Derek lifted the animal off my chest and set it on the floor. "Sorry about that."

"You have a cat?" I said. He did not seem like a cat person or a pet person of any sort.

"Yeah," he said. "Damn thing showed up one day and then kept showing up. So, I brought her in, not wanting her to be out and about causing a stray problem."

I raised an eyebrow.

"I was only thinking about the town," he said. "But I took her to the vet and got her fixed. Now she won't go away."

"She's in the house," I said. "How exactly is she supposed to go away?"

"She goes outside sometimes," he said. "I let her out in the backyard."

I nodded. "Your fenced-in backyard?"

"She's good company." He grinned sheepishly. "But if she bothers you too much, I can block her off during the day."

"No," I said. "That won't be necessary. She won't bother me at all. She seems nice." The cat perched on the windowsill overlooking the backyard. Her tail flicked back and forth.

"Yeah."

"And her name is Cat?" I asked.

He nodded and shrugged. "I couldn't think of anything else."

Cat yawned and stretched. She was orange, with white socks on all four paws. "It suits her."

"Yeah, I suppose." Derek checked his watch. "I've got to get back to the station, but if you need anything, just call me. Here are the TV remotes. Surf to your heart's content. If you find something you want to rent, feel free to do that, too."

A feeling of inadequacy settled in the pit of my stomach, but I nodded. "Thanks."

Derek left.

I stared at the black screen of the TV. Sure, I could rent something if I wanted to. But how would I pay for it? How was I going to pay for a lot of things? I lived comfortably, a single Omega renting half a house, but now I'd be a single Omega with a baby on the way, renting what? I wished I had a newspaper then to pull out the apartment ads for Millerstown.

I had plenty of free time on my hands to work out a new budget to try and accommodate the new direction my life was taking.

Chapter Six

Derek

Cam had been staying at the house for two weeks, and it was no easier to leave him when I went to work now than it had been that very first day, when he tried to pretend all was right with the world and that he was not in excruciating pain.

I was so glad to finally have my day off so that I could spend time with the Omega who had already wormed his way into my heart, despite my efforts to keep him out.

His pain had eased with time, and I'd convinced him to call his doctor, who basically told him to deal with it. Asshat. I knew that being pregnant meant a decrease in treatment options, but having none shocked me.

"So, no over-the-counter things or anything?" I grabbed a new pillow to place beneath his leg.

"They think it might be a risk given my test results—which they also assure me are fine." He rolled his eyes at the assness that was being homebound and in pain.

My phone buzzed, and a quick glance told me they were here. "Do you want a blanket? I have a delivery just about here, so the door will be open."

Little did he know, the delivery was for him. When I had some downtime, I googled the crap out of things that helped make having a leg injury less awful. The only thing that popped up in all my searches that I could make it happen was a recliner. If a new chair made his day easier, a new chair it was.

"I'm hurt, not old." He stuck his tongue out, and my mind flooded with things he could do with that tongue or that I could do with mine. I was worse than a teen, walking around with a boner all the time. He did that to me. Cam, his scent, his humor, his smile—all of it had a direct link to my cock. It was a love/hate thing if ever there was one.

"Fair enough." I made it to the door just as the truck pulled into the driveway. The two delivery guys carried the chair into the room and placed it beside the couch then left. The space had been empty before, and the new addition rounded out the room nicely.

"That looks nice," Cam said.

"Let me help you up?" I held out a hand.

"Why?" he asked, ignoring my offering.

"Don't you want to try your new chair?" I suppressed a grin.

He looked from me to the chair and back again, surprise then confusion passing over his face. "You bought me a chair?"

"Well, the couch hasn't been very comfortable for you. I know you didn't want me to notice, but I see you."

His jaw dropped as I told him I saw him. How had he not noticed? He was all I saw from the slight flinches of pain to the way his eyes looked just above me when he was nervous. I studied him, needing to see how he ticked, looking for that one sign that let me find a way into his life without steamrolling.

Sure, we had our child coming. But that only connected us as parents and, God help me, I wanted so much more.

"And so, you bought me a recliner?" He pushed himself to sit, swinging his leg over the edge of the couch, still ignoring my hand.

"That about sums it up." I shrugged.

"I can pay for it." He pushed himself up, and my heart soared that he was willing to push aside his obvious inner struggles with my gift and allow himself to be comfortable.

I stepped away, grabbed the dictionary off the shelf, and opened it. "Gift: a thing given freely," I read before closing and shelving it.

"Wise ass." He hobbled over to the recliner and sat down. It took all my restraint not to rush over and assist him, but Cam had already ignored my offer once, I didn't want another rejection.

"You love me," I sassed back, immediately regretting the awkwardness it created.

"Whateves." He fidgeted with the lever. "Help me get the legs up?"

I bent down and saw that there was a lock on the recliner for the delivery, so I removed the piece of plastic, allowing the chair to recline with ease.

"Your cast looks tight." Almost too tight." How had I missed that?

"I know." Cam sighed, "I called today, and the nurse said to come in at nine tomorrow, and we'll get a new cast or possibly my boot early."

"I'll drive you." Caveman Derek was officially in the house.

"I can get Toby to drive me. I already checked with him, and he's off work."

"Or I can drive you." I needed to hear what the doctor had to say. All this pain couldn't be good for our baby, and it sure as shit wasn't good for Cam.

"Are you always this stubborn?" He smirked. At least he found amusement in it instead of anger.

"I am with you. I just need you safe." The words fell out of my mouth — my filter so far gone.

"Because of the baby?" He tensed.

"No." I took his hand, kneeling beside the recliner. "I need the baby safe. Of that, have no doubt. But I need you safe, too. It's not even a choice anymore, and before you get weird about the old-guy stalkerness that sounded like, I'll never push you into anything."

"You are not old."

"Older than you." By a shit ton, not that I wanted to focus on that. We had enough obstacles in our way.

"You know what they say about men being like wine?" He winked, and the mood instantly lightened. Or at least shifted to more sexy than serious. "You are proof of that."

"Watch your words, Omega. You're going to give this Alpha ideas." Not that I needed any assistance in that department. Just thinking about the Omega in my home had me getting far more ideas than I should be having.

"At least then I won't be the only one."

He was officially trying to kill me. I leaned down, determined to kiss him, finally, but then my phone rang.

Chapter Seven

Cam

"Shit." Derek stood.

Disappointment spread through me, though I knew I shouldn't let it. It was good that we'd stopped before going any further.

My heart still pinged with joy at having gotten this gift from Derek. He cared about me, my comfort and that of our child. This gift was proof of that, and it meant so much.

While he was on the phone, I sank into the comfort of my new chair. Derek's chair. I was just borrowing it while I was here, laid up. I hadn't been able to move from the couch in two weeks, except to get up and piss or go to bed. And most of the time I needed help to accomplish either of those things. Some nights, I wondered why I even bothered having Derek help me to bed. Except I knew why, because when Derek helped me to bed, he practically carried me from the couch down the hall then placed me in the bed and tucked me in.

It was the only physical contact I got from him. And, though I wouldn't admit it out loud, I enjoyed it very much.

"What's going on?" I asked.

"We got a vandalism call from the city park. I better go check it out."

"Right now?" I said. "It's eight o'clock at night on a Friday."

"Yep," he said. "Sorry. Duty calls."

"I know," I said. "I understand. I am a firefighter."

He nodded. "Well, is there anything you need before I go?"

"No. I'm fine." I let out a frustrated sigh. My attitude was piss poor. I knew it, but I didn't let that stop me. Although it was unfair of me to take out my frustrations on Derek. It wasn't his fault my leg was broken. It wasn't his fault I was pregnant. Well, okay, so it kind of was, but I wasn't upset about that. It was just not in the plans I had for my life.

I rested my hand on my abdomen, still mostly flat. Although now that I knew I was pregnant, I could feel a slight curve, and every once in a while I felt a fluttering, but if I focused too hard on it, it went away.

My next Omega specialist appointment was in the next couple of days. I couldn't wait to find out more about our baby.

"Call me if you need anything, okay? You've got your phone? It's charged?"

"Yes," I said. "I'm fine."

"All right." He put his hands in the air. "Don't bite my head off."

"Don't ask me stupid questions."

He rolled his eyes and left the room. The front door shut a little more harshly than was necessary.

I flopped my head back on the pillow. Stupid. My behavior was stupid. I was a grown-ass man, not a child. I didn't need to treat Derek like this, especially after he'd just gotten me this chair. I'd apologize when he came back. Derek had opened up to me, showed me he cared, and how did I react? By being an ass.

I was just so frustrated and bored. Every day I sat here, watching the news, browsing Netflix. I'd read several books. I'd taken to becoming the neighborhood watch. Derek had his house equipped with security cameras, one on the porch, one inside that showed the entryway, one on the rear deck that showed a full view of the fenced backyard, and one in the kitchen facing the side entry of the garage. They were equipped with motion detection as well. So, the minute any motion was detected, it sent an alert to his phone. Last week, he'd set it up so that it alerted my phone as well. I always knew when the mail was coming, or if anyone walked by, or if there was a squirrel in the backyard. I spent more time than was normal watching the view because there wasn't much else to do.

Cat hopped onto my lap. She purred contentedly as she made a bed for herself on my hip. I scratched behind her ears as I scrolled through my phone. There were several motion detections from the day. I watched each of them — by the fifth one I started to get a little concerned. The same person dressed in a pair of jeans, a ball cap, and sunglasses walked by the house just about every fifteen minutes, first going one way then the next, then back again.

The last time the individual had walked by was an hour ago. Was it a bored teenager? That didn't make any sense. It was a Friday night. Surely a bored teenager would find something better to do. *Like vandalize the city park.*

A new notification came in, this time for the backyard. I clicked on it. As I was waiting for it to pull up, I looked out the window. I couldn't see anything because the shades were down, and it was dark outside. The light switch that would illuminate the deck was across the room. I was helpless. Just like I'd been for the past two weeks.

I couldn't wait for the doctor to give me the go ahead to start moving, but they hadn't liked the way my leg was healing the last time we went in, so they'd waited to put the boot on. Hopefully, tomorrow, they'd finally get me out of this itchy cast.

The video clip came up on my phone. The deck illuminated with the night-vision capabilities of the camera. My breath caught when I realized what I was watching. The gate swung open, and a figure emerged. A young man, wearing jeans, and a ball cap, came into the backyard. The same one who'd been walking past the house an hour prior.

Casing the place? Waiting for the owner to leave so he could break in and rob the place? We didn't get many break-ins in Millerstown, but they weren't beyond the realm of possibility. Or was it Nick coming back for some revenge? Derek had said he was keeping an eye out, though I thought it was unnecessary. What would Nick want with me?

I switched over to the live view. The man went from being in the backyard to being on the deck.

"Fuck." The shades were drawn, so he couldn't see in. He appeared to be trying the window in the back room just off the garage. Thankfully, Derek was a police officer and kept his house locked down like Fort Knox, despite the fact this was Millerstown and crime was fairly low.

I called his phone. It rang and rang, and then went to voicemail. "Fuck."

I needed to hide, and fast. It's not as if I could run. We'd brought my car here. But hell, I didn't even know where Derek had put the keys. I hadn't driven it, wasn't even sure if it was full of gas or not.

I grabbed the crutches propped against the wall and got to my feet. My legs got tangled in the blanket. In making myself comfortable with a pile blankets and pillows, I had made it difficult to move quickly.

Cat hopped off the couch, her tail flicking furiously. She growled and hissed; her hair stood on end as she looked at the window. I stood still, watching a shadowy figure move from one end of the deck to the other.

"Fuck," I whispered again and moved as quickly as I could.

I crutched down the hall, unsure where exactly I planned on hiding, but I assumed the master bedroom was my best bet. I found my phone again as I got in the room and clicked the lock on the door. Derek answered on the second ring this time.

"I was just about to call you back. What's up?"

"Someone's here," I said. "Trying to break in."

"What?"

"They're on the back deck right now."

"I'm turning around," Derek said. "Where are you?"

"I'm in your bedroom."

"Good. Lock the door. See if you can prop something against it. The dresser, maybe. I keep a handgun in the safe next to my bed. The code is two-three-two-nine."

"All right," I said. "Hurry."

"I will. I'll be right there. Put the phone down but stay on the line. I'll radio in to dispatch."

"All right." I paused. "Derek. I'm scared." I hated to admit it. It made me feel like less of a man, but dammit, that was the truth. I had a broken leg and a baby on the way, and there was a man breaking into my safe place.

"I know, baby," he said. "I'll be right there."

Through the phone, I heard the sirens go off. I turned my volume down. I didn't need to alert this guy as to where I was. Keeping the call active, I switched to the view of the surveillance cameras.

The guy was still on the back deck, trying to pick the lock. I wished there was some sort of siren I could turn on that would scare him off, or I could go out there, guns blazing. What good would that do me, though? I wasn't the best shot, and I didn't know what sort of weapon he had, if any. And I had a baby to think about. Maybe if I wasn't pregnant, I would take that risk, but I couldn't now.

I got the handgun from Derek's safe then hid in his closet. I put as many barriers between me and the guy outside as I possibly could. In the time it took me to get the gun and hide, the guy had managed to move from the deck, and was no longer visible on any of the cameras. It didn't appear the back door was open, though, so he wasn't in the house. I didn't think.

I toggled between the deck camera and the inside one. No movement, except for Cat growling at the front door. Fuck. Would she listen to me if I went out there to get her? Was it worth the risk?

Damn it.

"Cam? Are you still there?" Derek's voice was distant, and I realized I was still on the phone.

"Yeah," I said. "I'm here. I'm in your bedroom."

"Good. I'm pulling onto the street. Where is the guy?"

"I don't know," I said. "He's not in the house. At least I don't think he is. Maybe he left?" I tapped on my screen then and went to the camera that faced the front door. "He's on the porch," I said. "He's trying to get in that door. He's looking for a key, maybe?"

"All right. I'll be right there." Derek said.

I heard the sirens louder now, letting everyone know Derek was coming up the road. Then I saw his car whip into the driveway.

The man on the porch took off on foot. Derek jumped from the car and followed. That's when I lost visual of both of them. The immediate danger was gone for me, and I was relieved. I put a hand over my stomach, and my heart rate slowed.

"It's going to be fine, baby. We're going to be okay." Jesus. I hadn't realized how much my heart rate had increased. Now that the adrenaline slowed, my leg began to throb. Though the threat was gone for me, Derek was still out there.

"Fuck." I hung up the phone so I could call Jeffries. He could come provide some backup to Derek.

It felt like hours between me calling and help arriving. Meanwhile, Derek was out there risking his life for me and our child. I stood in the front entryway, as two more police cruisers came down the road and parked at the curb. Jeffries and Connor, one of the younger officers, stepped out.

Derek returned, out of breath. He shook his head. "That son of a bitch is fast."

Jeffries already had his phone out. "I'll call for more backup, we'll put a BOLO out on him. We can get a picture off your cameras."

"Thanks," Derek said.

He stepped on to the porch and pulled me into his arms.

I relaxed against him, surprising at how easy it was to do so. "Are you okay?" I asked

"Yeah." He squeezed me tighter. "Never been so scared in my life. Never driven so fast, either. You sure you're all right?"

My panic subsided as my Alpha held me, the safety of his embrace calming. I laughed wryly. "Sure, nothing like an attempted breaking and entering to get the blood pumping."

Chapter Eight

Derek

It took everything I had in me to go to work the next morning. I'd settled Cam in my room for the night and lain awake next to him for hours before succumbing to sleep. That morning, I'd awoken with him in my arms.

I'd helped him to his chair, made sure he was stocked up with everything he needed for the day. I also vowed to call him every half hour for the rest of the day.

"Just go." Cam had smiled. "You can't catch the guy if you're here with me." Little did he know that Turner and his Omega, Kayden, would be visiting throughout the day.

And so I went.

"Millerstown is going to hell in a handbasket." Toby rolled his eyes as he mimicked the older woman who came in to complain about her neighbor leaving the trash bin out all week.

Of course, the topic we were discussing today was far more serious than a trash bin.

It was the safety of my family. Cam and our child shouldn't need to be hanging out with Turner and his Omega so I could have a fucking meeting at work. That should not be his existence.

"Har har, Mrs. Fines." I threw a wad of paper at his head.

"Rita is on her way." Toby wheeled in the coffee cart. The man was officially a genius. Of course, we had more than just our crew at this meeting, and we needed to make a good impression. Jeffries had gone out of his way to make this task force one that would result in finding the asshat and fast.

I owed him so much.

Looking around the room, I took a quick head count. Only Rita and Jeffries were missing, and since Jeffries was watching my Omega, it was only Rita. I crossed my fingers there were no calls coming in. This was too freaking important to be interrupted by someone wanting us to check out the person who tried to sell them a vacuum because of course they were a serial killer and not some poor schlub hoping to make some commission.

"Sorry, had to get these." Rita brought in a tray of donuts from the bakery across the way. How cliché. And utterly perfect.

"We can start. Jeffries will not be joining us today." I turned on the laptop and projected the best picture we had of the slime ball. "This is Nick Graham, or at least Nick Graham five years ago." All I had was his expired driver's license.

I inhaled deeply. This next part was going to be horrible for me to get through without showing my emotions. I wanted to break shit and call for blood like some caveman. Instead, I needed to calmly explain the situation to the people who worked under me.

Not as if they didn't already know. The department was tiny, as was the town.

"Last night, Nick showed up at my place, with his eyes on getting to Cameron McNeil. He was seen on surveillance casing my place and only minutes after I left, he attempted to — we are assuming enact some sort of revenge for the death of Drew Burns."

Heads nodded in understanding. Knowing this place, they had already read the report and Connor had probably circled the grammar errors. To be "helpful" and not a pain in the ass, of course.

"Jeffries is currently with Cameron, keeping him safe, but that is a short-term solution. We need to find him."

"Rita says we are getting outside help," Toby chimed in.

Because Rita is an eavesdropper extraordinaire.

"Yes, as part of our new task force dealing with the meth issue, we are receiving assistance." Thanks to Jeffries' connections.

"So, what is the long term plan for your Omega?" Ned had been trying to get me going on that since he saw me leave the bar with Cam. At first, I thought he was being an ass, but as time progressed I had become more convinced it was his way of trying to help me find my happily ever after. If only it were that easy.

Cam was having my baby while sporting a broken leg and having to worry about a crazy man after him. Nothing about that was ideal except the baby part. I was so excited to be a father.

This wasn't the way I had planned on it happening, but in my heart, I knew Cam was the one, so timing was just that — timing. If he decided to let me, I planned to be the best Alpha he could ever ask for.

Problem was getting him to let me.

"Chief?"

Of fuck. I couldn't afford to get lost in my head like that. Not with Cam's safety on the line.

"I don't know. Jeffries and I are meeting about that after we're done here." Which I wanted to end right then. Not being with Cam had me a nervous wreck. "I collected all the pertinent info, so if we could hold off questions until I finish, that might work best."

That wasn't how we generally worked as a group, but this was too personal, and fear of messing things up had me following old-school management styles or whatever the heck they called my job in bigger cities. It took me twenty minutes to go through all we knew about Nick. We didn't know much and that was killing me. He did have a sister a few counties over, and while she insisted she hadn't seen him, we had sent their local precinct to check. Maybe we would get lucky.

We could really use some luck. Millerstown couldn't afford to supply us with the fancy equipment and staffing of bigger cities. Our data collection was weak at best. That was something I planned to discuss with Jeffries and Harrison to improve in the future. There had to be a better way for us to be connected to the information we needed without hemorrhaging money or having bake sales at every traffic stop.

"Other than that," I concluded, "just be vigilant. That's all we can do."

Everyone headed straight to the donuts, because donuts, and I was able to worm my way out of there. I had come in on my day off because we needed to get everyone up to date, but now I just needed to find Jefferies and my Omega.

I made the short drive home and texted Jeffries from outside. I needed to talk to him before I saw Cam. I wanted to have a plan in place, so I didn't want to go to Cam with a *doing our best* with no plan in place. He deserved better than that.

"Hey." Jeffries stepped outside and clicked the door shut behind him. "Any word?"

I gave a slight shake of my head and leaned against the wall. "Not really. So far, the plan is catch the bad guy and keep my Omega safe."

Jeffries' arm came around me. "I get it. I so very much get it. And know this—we will get him." I appreciated his words and the sincerity he used while speaking them. He believed all would be right, and I had to as well.

"I don't want to ever leave him," I confessed. "It's like—like..."

"Like when he isn't there, part of you isn't either," he finished my thoughts.

"What are you, psychic?" I gave him a playful smack and stepped out from under his arm.

"Yeah something like that. Or I just know exactly what you're going through." He rolled his eyes. Big tough Jeffries rolled his eyes. "I have an idea I think your Omega will like far more than you do."

Which meant I was going to fucking hate it. But I trusted Jeffries, and if he thought it would keep Cam safe, I was willing to give it a go.

"Hit me with it."

"Cam goes back to work part-time and takes the same shifts you work, so he isn't home alone."

Okay, maybe I wasn't willing to give it a go.

"That is ludicrous. He can barely stand on his own, he still may need surgery, and the station is open to the public," and that was just the beginning of the ever-growing list in my mind.

"Think about it."

"I have. I am on nights for a while, and there is no way that would be good for our baby. Let's catch this bastard before I rotate back to days. We can just make sure people are here with him." Cam was very much not going to love that although he had been scared — so very scared that night, so maybe he would concede.

"And on nights there isn't anyone available, he can come to my place. We have a bedroom he could use."

As much as I hated the idea of him not being under my roof, that had merit.

"You don't worry about him coming to your place?" I asked, already pretty sure I knew the answer. Jeffries would never allow anything to put his family, including his extended family, in danger.

"This guy is trying to get to Cam while he is alone, and his running away means he wants to come out of this alive. Cam will be safe as long as he is with others."

I trusted Jefferies' opinions on these things, even if what I truly wanted was to be glued to Cam's side.

"Let's go in. The little eavesdropper looks like he has things to say." He tilted his head toward the open window just as Cam's head snapped back.

He was sure going to keep me on my toes.

Inside, Cam was leaning against the wall pretending he was just chilling as Jeffries went to the other room to be with Kayden and Jackson.

"How was your day?" I asked.

He laughed, which I found encouraging. "It was surprisingly good. Kayden's always a blast to hang out with, and Jackson is hilarious. We played a lot of card games and binge watched some really odd kid shows."

"Good," I said. "I'm glad. So how much of my conversation did you hear?" I asked getting into his space. The man was a freaking magnet, and not being pressed against him always took a lot of willpower.

"I do want to go back to work. I don't need a babysitter, but it isn't only me now, so I will accept them. And you get all cave manny about me." His voice softened, and the tiny bit of restraint I felt slipped away.

"I wish you would wait for the doctor to clear you." I closed the distance between us and opened my arms. When he stepped into them, well, hobbled into them, all was right with the world, even if only for that split second.

"Done." He settled his head against my chest.

"I can't help the cave manny crap," I confessed, not sure I wanted to help it anyway.

"That's okay. I kind of like it." He tilted his head up, his eyes on my lips and it was all the invitation I needed. I brushed my lips against his, only to be interrupted by Jefferies' son asking if they could come back tomorrow and if he could have some more hot chocolate before he left.

"Sure, Jack. We can make that happen," I said.

The kid beamed.

I scooped Cam up and carried him into the kitchen. If he wanted caveman, I could give him caveman. I was beginning to realize there was nothing I wouldn't give the man and the kiss I pressed to his lips, however brief, had me confident that one day he was going to let me.

Chapter Nine

Cam

"What about this one?" I pointed at the fourth crib of the afternoon. We were at a big box store that specialized in infant furniture and other baby items we'd need. So far, we were only shopping for one set of items. We hadn't yet figured out the living situation. Sure, I could look up apartments, but then I'd have to face the reality of looking up apartments. Or reality of my feelings for Derek and how I wondered how I'd live without him by my side each night.

"I like it," Derek said. "I want to run a check on it, though, to make sure there are no recalls."

"It wouldn't be in the store if there were," I protested.

"Maybe, but we should at least look to see how other people like it."

"It's a crib. What's there to complain about? The crib is fine. It looks sturdy. Put a mattress in it, set the baby down, we're done."

"There's more to it than that," Derek said. "We can't pick just any crib. It has to be perfect."

"Well, if we're only picking out perfect items, we're going to be here for a while. And also, we're going to go broke. Both of us are city employees, you know."

"Yeah," he said. "That's true."

In the end, we put it on the list of items we'd probably end up getting. We were just browsing right now anyway. We hadn't yet selected a theme for the nursery or a room. Derek had one guest room and a workout room, but I was currently living in the guest room, though I wasn't actually staying there most of the time. Or ever. I kept my clothes in that closet, though, because if I kept my stuff next to Derek's in his closet, then there would be no denying the ways in which our relationship had changed.

Today was the first time in a while that Derek had let me out of the house for something other than work. I think he sensed I was about to go stir crazy if I had to stay inside any longer.

"What kind of color scheme should we do?" I asked. "The guest room is painted a nice blue, but the office is beige. Guess it doesn't really matter. We can make anything go with those colors, right?"

Derek shrugged. "That's not really my area of expertise."

I snorted. "Me neither."

We browsed around the store a while longer, and I got overwhelmed by just how much stuff there was for children. For example, an entire twenty-by- eight-foot display of bottles. Just bottles. Different sizes, nipple shapes, colors. I couldn't even fathom how I was going to choose between them. I guess I would add it to my list of things to research while I was laid up.

"Do these things come with manuals?" I stared at the wall of diapers and all of the table, pails, and other junk that went along with them.

"What? The diaper pail things?"

"No, babies."

"I don't think so," Derek said. "Pretty sure it's a learn-as-you-go situation. Sink or swim."

I grimaced.

"We'll be just fine." He wrapped his arm around my waist. "You'll do great."

With him by my side, keeping me steady, I almost believed it. "I hope so."

I thumbed through the books that they had available, focusing on an Omega pregnancy volume with lots of illustrations and helpful diagrams. I skimmed a few of the pages then set it back on the shelf. Derek picked it up and put it in the cart. He did the same with the next book I looked at.

"You don't have to get those," I said.

"I don't mind." He grinned, and my stomach flipped. "I know you enjoy reading, and if you if you think it's something useful, then consider it a gift."

I didn't feel like arguing, and I wasn't exactly in a place where I could be shelling out extra money for things I could do without. Derek was still getting a paycheck, though so I guessed I wouldn't mind. Just this once.

We left the baby store with way more items than I'd anticipated purchasing. I got the books that I had picked up, as well as a Diaper Genie we'd found on sale, a high chair, and an oversized stuffed feline that oddly resembled Cat. I held it in my hands as we drove to the restaurant we were going to for lunch.

"You think Cat will like this?" I asked. "It looks a lot like her."

"She's an orange tabby. Every orange cat looks like her."

"Still," I said. "It's going to be funny. I can't wait to see her reaction."

"Me, too." Derek chuckled.

It was so easy to be with him, to spend time with him day in and day out. Was this what normal relationships were like? I could imagine having one of those with Derek someday.

We pulled into the restaurant, a local diner called Bowman's, owned by Harrison, the mayor. It served breakfast all day, which made it the best place around.

"Pancakes sound really good," I said. "Don't you think?"

"I'm going to get me a burger," he said. "With lots of greasy fries."

I wrinkled my nose. "I want pancakes and hash browns and eggs. Maybe some sausage, too."

Derek raised an eyebrow. "Did you skip breakfast?"

"No," I said. "Just hungry."

We went in and sat down. A few minutes later Turner and Kayden came in. I waved them over to our table. "Hey, guys, what are you doing out and about?"

"Well, we were going to head home, but Kayden saw this place and figured he could use some breakfast food."

Kayden rested his hand on his large belly. "I'm going to take advantage of eating for two while I can. I recommend you do the same, Cam."

"Oh, I am," I said. "I'm getting the Alpha breakfast special."

"Oh!" Kayden slid into the booth and picked up the menu. "What's that?"

"It includes pretty much everything."

"I want one of those." Kayden put the menu back down without even looking at it.

Turner sat down next to him. "Maybe we should tell Harrison to rename it the Pregnant Omega special."

He had the decency to look sheepish when Kayden and I both glared at him.

"So, did you guys get everything you needed at the baby store?" Turner asked.

I looked up at him. "How do you know that's where we went?"

"We drove by and saw your car."

I narrowed my eyes. Something wasn't adding up.

"Oh, for goodness sake, Turner. You call yourself an FBI agent?" Kayden threw his hands in the air and turned to me. "Derek didn't like the idea of the two of you being out and about with him as your only protection. Turner and I were essentially backup. Although I have no idea what I was going to do if he had to take off in pursuit."

"Really, Derek? Do you think that was necessary?" I asked.

"I wasn't taking any chances," he said. "And Turner was supposed to stay out of the way not show up for lunch."

Turner shrugged. "Hey, I've got a hungry Omega to feed, too."

"Well," I said, "I hope it wasn't too boring for you guys. It was completely unnecessary. It's bad enough you're babysitting me every other day. This should be your day off."

Kayden shrugged. "We were happy to do it. It was nice to get out of the house. Ollie has Jackson, and we needed to pick up a few things for this little lady anyway. Plus, I'm getting breakfast out of the deal, so that's nice, too."

"Yeah, I suppose it is. But, next time, don't listen to this guy." I jerked my thumb toward Derek. "He worries too much."

Derek lifted his arm and put it around the back of the booth. "There's no such thing as worrying to much when it comes to your family. Just trying to keep you safe, Omega."

Turner nodded. "I second that."

I grinned. I supposed I couldn't complain since my Alpha was just being helpful and protective.

Chapter Ten

Cam

"So then, we figured if you had actually been there, Philip and I wouldn't have had to carry this unconscious six-foot-four dude by ourselves." Bobby laughed as he took another swig of his drink.

It was nice to have my friends over, even if they were here to just babysit me. It had been too long since we hung out outside of work. Philip and Ollie, with their brand new daughter McKenna, as well as Bobby from the crew, came over with pizzas while Derek was on night shift.

"That's crazy," I said. "Don't worry, though. I'll be back on duty soon."

"Oh yeah?" Bobby said. "Wasn't sure what your plans were once the little one arrives. Are they taking that cast off soon?"

I nodded. "Next couple of days, I think. We had an appointment last week that we canceled after the attempted break-in, but I go back soon. Then I can start walking around again. It'll be a while before I run into any burning buildings, though." I rubbed a hand absently over my belly.

Ollie chuckled. "Yeah. I can't even imagine running after anyone while pregnant."

"Me neither," I said. "Not only would it be completely unsafe, but good lord, I'm not sure which is more difficult, navigating with a broken leg or this big belly." I wasn't even that big yet, but I felt like in the three weeks since breaking my leg my stomach had doubled in size.

"You'll be going back to full duty after the baby is born, though?" Ollie asked.

"I'm hoping to. Derek and I haven't talked about it much."

Ollie nodded. "Well, Kayden and I have been talking, and we figured we can try and work out a schedule so that we can cover daycare while you are on the job. We can deal with your shifts and Derek's."

I raised my eyebrows. "You'd be willing to do that? You know I work three on two off."

"Yeah." He shrugged. "It won't be any different than watching the other daycare kids. Just different hours. I've got McKenna, but she'll be much older by the time your baby is here. That way you can return to work, and we'll have another kid at daycare."

"That would be awesome," I said. "Derek and I both have some family in town, but I wasn't sure how we'd make it work. My mom works full time, but she's already said she'd love to watch the baby when she can."

"We'll get something worked out," Ollie said. "That's what we do within the department. We're family."

"Thanks." Just like that, another worry was lifted off my shoulders. I'd had no idea how we were going to work that out. I'd been avoiding thinking about it, honestly. Derek had brought it up a few times, but I'd told him I didn't want to discuss it quite yet. I couldn't quite bring myself to worry about another thing.

"Do you think you'll stay here or—?"

Ollie sent an elbow into Philip's ribs. "That's none of our business."

I laughed nervously. "I don't know. We haven't talked about it yet."

"Hell, the way Derek put it at the task force meeting the other day made it sound like you wouldn't be leaving his sight ever again. I was kind of surprised that he goes to work," Bobby put in.

"What?" I was stunned.

"The task force they put together to find that Alpha, Nick Graham."

"Yeah," I said. "What about it?"

"Apparently, they had a big meeting with the state police as well as some guys from Rochdale. Chief laid down the law. He wants this guy found before he can get near you ever again. Everybody's on the lookout. Police take care of their own."

Derek had mentioned that they were actively searching for Nick. But he hadn't made it sound so dramatic.

"What did he say?" I asked.

Bobby shrugged. "Just that they were looking for Nick to make sure he didn't get you and how you are a poor, defenseless Omega, all cooped up in the house with your broken leg and a baby on the way. A little Omega in distress."

I picked up one of my paperbacks and tossed it at Bobby. "Shut up." I could handle the ribbing, I'd taken it for a long time, being the only Omega at the fire department. But damn, I didn't want to have to deal with Derek talking about me like that behind my back. Sure, I was laid up with a baby on the way, but I wasn't helpless. Nick hadn't even gotten in the house the last time and, if he had, I would have been ready to defend myself.

Damn Derek and his meddling. I may be an Omega, but that didn't make me useless.

Philip shook his head. "Don't listen to him, Cam. Everybody's just worried about this guy being on the loose. He's probably got it out for you since you turned him in and his dumbass Omega died blowing up the house."

"Yeah," I said. "I know."

"So," he said, "you bored out of your mind yet?"

"Fuck yes, I have been bored for weeks now," I groaned. "I'm running out of shows to watch, things to read. I'm about ready to pull the dictionary off the shelf and read that."

Philip chuckled. "Well, I might have something that can help you. Harrison has some plans for building town morale. He noticed that the softball game did a lot of good, bringing us all together after what happened with my dad. He wants to do more things like that. Some events could potentially be used as fundraisers for the school or food drives or whatever."

I perked up. "Sounds interesting. What can I do to help?"

"Well, he wants the police and fire departments to be in on the planning, as well as some of the other businesses in town. Problem is, there's a lot of paperwork involved. Organization, planning, coordinating. Not a lot of us have time for that. We're still recovering financially from what my dad did.

I knew Philip had taken his dad's actions pretty hard. No one had blamed him, though. His dad had laundered money and nearly driven the town to bankruptcy, but it wasn't Philip's fault.

"What do you need?" I said.

He pulled a file folder from the ginormous diaper bag Ollie had brought in with them. "Take a look at what we've put together. So far, we've just brainstormed ideas. But what we'd like to do is have some events planned throughout the year. A few big ones, maybe once a quarter, and then smaller ones sprinkled throughout." He handed me another file folder. "I also wanted to see if you wouldn't mind handling the scheduling at the fire department. It'd be nice if you could take that over. It'll be part of your new responsibilities once you get that promotion anyway. Might as well learn it now."

"Really?" I said, eyebrows raised. "I'll still get it, even in my condition?"

"You know we can't discriminate based on that, and we wouldn't ever anyway. You're a good fireman. You deserve it."

I smiled. "Thanks, Philip. I'll take a look at these as soon as I can. I'd kick you all right now, but I'm not done with my pizza." I set the folders on my ever-growing pile of things on the table next to me.

McKenna, who was bundled carefully in a swaddle blanket in her Omega dad's arms, let out a soft cry. Ollie balanced her with one hand while eating a slice of pizza with the other.

"You want me to take her?" I said. "I can hold on to her."

"You don't mind?"

"I need the practice." I held my arms out, and Ollie handed the baby to me.

I put the footrest down so I could rock in the chair instead of having it sit still. McKenna blinked her little eyes at me for a moment, then she must have deemed me to be trustworthy enough because they fluttered closed and didn't open again as I softly rocked her.

"You want to come over at two in the morning and do that?" Philip asked.

"Nope," I said. "Not yet. I'll be doing that, too, in due time, though. Don't you worry."

After a while, McKenna got to fussing enough that Ollie had to take her back and get her home. Try as I might to soothe her, I wasn't her Omega dad. Having a little baby in my arms, though, made me ache to meet my own child.

Despite the circumstances, I knew Derek and I would be good parents. We'd be able to work together for the good of our child. Whether we were *together* or not was another story. As each day passed, I wanted to be together more and more, experience another kiss like the one a few days ago.

Derek wasn't due home until midnight or possibly later. Sometimes he stayed a while after his shift to get paperwork done. I was able to move around a lot better now that my leg was healing, and I crutched my way down the hall. Since the attack at the house, I'd been sleeping in his room even though I usually had a babysitter downstairs, one of the guys on the force or the fire department staying over.

I didn't need him to protect me per se, but it most certainly didn't hurt. It surprised me how much I missed his warmth when it wasn't there. I climbed into the bed and under the covers, resting my head on a pillow that smelled of my Alpha. Cat leapt onto the bed as well, and she slept on my hip like she liked to do, purring softly.

I woke up hours later, when Derek arrived home. He came in the bedroom, took off his belt, put away his service weapon, and began undressing.

"How was your shift?" I asked. "Anything exciting happen?"

"Couple of speeders," he said. "And some teenagers out past curfew."

"You ought to just let them be." I chuckled. "You were young once, weren't you?"

"Yeah," he said. "Which is why I sent them home. I know what kind of trouble they can get into if I let them stay out on the streets."

"Spoilsport."

"Yeah, maybe." He rubbed the back of his neck.

"Everything all right?"

"Yeah, I just wish we were able to find that damn Alpha. I don't like having him out there."

"You'll find him." I rolled my eyes. "And, you know, I really don't appreciate you portraying me as some sort of Omega in distress who needs you to swoop in and save me."

"What? Where'd you get that idea?" he asked, sitting on the bed and looking at me.

I sat up. "The guys came to visit, and apparently they've been razzing on me a bit behind my back about how my big bad Alpha has a task force out there looking for Nick."

"Geesh." Derek winced. "I'm sorry about that. I'm just trying to do my job." Clearly not sorry at all.

"You can do your job without making a sound like I'm some sort of princess in a castle waiting for you to rescue me. I already feel like a weirdo having to be babysat every minute of every day. Are we sure this is necessary?"

"Can we talk about this in the morning?" Derek said. "You know I don't feel that way. You know I think you're perfectly capable. Hell, you're the best fireman this town has. Philip says so all the time. You're more than capable of taking care of yourself. I want to catch this guy because he broke the law, and he threatened my Omega and unborn child. It scares me that he's out there, Cam. He's out there, and he's after you and our child."

I softened at that. I'd read Derek all wrong, jumped to conclusions completely off the mark. The vulnerability in what Derek was saying hit me. I covered his hand with mine. "I'm sorry," I said. "I'm being ungrateful. You're right. We do want to get him put him behind bars where he belongs. I'm scared, too. Scared that even though I'm perfectly capable of protecting myself, I won't be able to protect our child. I'd never forgive myself if something happened to him or her."

We each laid a hand over my abdomen.

"You're good dad," Derek said.

He leaned forward and pressed his lips to mine. The kiss lingered for a moment. Then he put his forehead to mine and took a deep breath, inhaling my scent.

My Alpha.

"Come on," he said. "Let's get some rest. I don't have to work till noon tomorrow, so we can sleep in."

I grinned. "That sounds nice." I settled back down on the bed. This time I laid my head on Derek's chest. I fell asleep easily, completely safe and content in my Alpha's arms.

Chapter Eleven

Derek

"Two doctor's appointments in one day." Cam talked to himself as he combed his hair.

I stood in the doorway watching him. As much as he was complaining, I knew he was excited for the day. Sure, being poked and prodded at stank, but by the end of the day he would finally get that blasted cast off and we would get to see our baby.

"Morning," I announced myself, feeling a bit too voyeurish for my own good.

"I was going to let you sleep." He blushed slightly, and I had a feeling he knew I overheard him.

He was embarrassed that I kept hearing him jabber away at himself, but to me having him feel comfortable enough here to do so felt like a victory.

"It's a big day." I came up behind him, taking the comb from his hand and running it through his hair. He could easily do it himself. And the first time I did this he told me as much. He had grown to accept it for what it was—me wanting to be close to him.

I didn't even have a hair thing. The first day he had been struggling with his balance and I wanted to make his life a little bit easier. The intimacy of the simple act was what I craved, and I had a feeling he did as well.

"What if they say I need another cast?" He leaned back into me. I got it. He wasn't healing as quickly as they wanted even with the massive amount of calcium, they were shoving at him.

"They won't. Last time they said it was close to being ready. Your body is so busy being the perfect provider for our child it is just taking longer to get to you. It's kind of a dad thing." I tried to lighten it with a joke, but instead of a chuckle, he let out a sigh. "What's weighing on you?" I asked, now knowing it was something more.

"What if it doesn't get better? What if this stupid leg means no more fighting fires?" He rotated in my arms and held onto me as if his life depended on my embrace. "I am a firefighter. I don't know how to be anything else."

I placed a kiss on the top of his head, wishing I could take it all away.

"The doctor never once hinted at anything but a full recovery, love." The pet name fell from my lips and, while it was true, I did love him, we had never said the words. Shit, with the exception of a few brief kisses, we had been nowhere near "I love you" land.

"And if we get bad news today?" He face was pained, his jaw clenched as he tried to hold back his emotions. Seeing strong Cam so broken and defeated crushed me.

"Then we will figure it out. You and me."

His head popped up as his eyes sought mine, his jaw dropped. What a horrible Alpha I'd been for him not to know that I was his. "Did you think I found your worth in your profession?"

He flinched but shook his head — barely.

"Oh, sweet sexy fierce Omega mine, I am with you for as long as you will have me in any way you will have me. If you want a co-parent — I'm there. A best friend — I'm there. A lover — I'm there. An everything — I'm there." I held his face in my hands, needing him to hear the sincerity of my words.

"You and me, we are in this together, if you are a firefighter or a stay-at-home father or you decide to become the town fundraiser. Your job does not define you," I set one of my hands on his chest above his heart. "This defines you…" I moved my hand to his head. "And this. You are the kindest, smartest, most amazing man I have ever met. I wish you could see yourself through my eyes."

He opened his mouth to speak, and I took it as an invitation, slamming my lips to his and kissing him with all the passion I had building up inside of me. When his tongue swiped my bottom lip, I deepened the kiss, needing to taste more of him.

If it weren't for the stupid alarm going off in the background, I have stayed there like that all morning.

"We have to go," he spoke, his breath labored from our kiss. "Dr. Shapiro squeezed me in. Or else…" He closed his eyes and stood there, not moving for what felt like ages, but was more like ten seconds. "I want everything." It was almost too quiet to hear.

"Me, too, Omega. Me, too."

We raced to the doctor's, getting there just in time to check in. We were called back almost immediately.

They had the X-rays taken quickly, and we were herded back to an exam room.

"The X-ray tech sure didn't give anything away," he grumbled as we watched the clock on the wall in the exam room. Early in didn't equate with early seen. "Usually I can kind of read them."

"It's going to be fine." I shimmied onto the exam table sideways, beside him. "You can always talk to me about anything, you know, right?"

"I know this now. I think I was just too afraid to believe it before."

I wrapped my arm around his shoulder and pulled him into my side. "Believe it." I kissed his head just as there was a knock on the door followed by the doctor coming inside with two nurses. "Let's get this bad boy off."

Within an hour, the cast was off, a boot was on, good news about a full recovery was given, and a follow up visit scheduled. It was the best ortho visit yet, and if it weren't for the boot, I had a feeling Cam would be skipping.

"Celebrate?" he asked as we reached the car.

"And by celebrate you mean?"

"The Pregnant Omega special, of course." He kissed me far too briefly before climbing into the passenger seat.

I drove to the diner, and since it was between mealtimes, the place was dead. We sat at a table, me setting a chair up for him to elevate his foot.

"Coffee?" Sally, the waitress set down two glasses of water and two straws.

"Please." I never turned down coffee unless it was that foo-foo stuff with butter. I liked my coffee good and strong, no sweetener or cream.

"No thanks." Cam's hand settled on his ever-growing belly. What smallness he'd had in the beginning of his pregnancy he more than made up for as time went on. He had gotten past that *too much pizza or baby* stage. He was stunning.

"Decaf?" She gave him a wink.

"I'd rather drink Moxie." He rolled his eyes as she gave a nod of agreement.

"Don't remind me of that stuff," she grumbled and scampered off to get my coffee.

"Moxie?" I'd heard the phrase but never used it in terms of a beverage before.

"A trucker who comes through here regularly and is sweet on her gave her a bottle. I guess it is a New England thing. Well, she took a sip and turned her head to spit it out" — he raised his voice—"all over the back of my head."

"It tastes like burnt root beer and rust mixed with bubble-gum-flavored pain reliever." She sauntered over with my coffee. "Anyone who kept that in their mouth deserved a fucking medal."

"He drank it down just fine," Cam teased back.

"And just for that I am going to ask Klyde to make your pancakes a tiny bit too small." She pointed her pen at me., "Cheeseburger today?"

"You know me so well."

"I know all you guys in uniform well. You all eat out too much." And just like that, she was off.

"Gotta love Sally." Cam smiled so bright. It was amazing seeing him having fun. I hadn't realized how worried he'd been over his leg. I needed to start paying better attention. I owed it to him to be the best Alpha I could be. Especially now that he was more receptive of me taking on that role.

"Don't you need to drink a ton of water for the ultrasound?" I pointed to his still-full glass.

"Nope. I totally lucked out. I am past the time you need to drink an entire buttload of water."

"Buttload being the official term."

"Exactly, and because they took an ultrasound at the hospital when I broke my leg, the doctor decided to wait for my 'official' one until now. Boom." He took a tiny sip of water. "See? All done."

I barked out a laugh, and not the first one during the meal. The food was amazing, but nowhere near as amazing as the company. We stayed and chatted long after the last bite was eaten, leaving only when we needed to make our way to the doctor's.

"Was it me, or did that feel like a date?" I asked as we walked into the office building.

"It was definitely a date." He gave me the side eye paired with a smirk. "Do you know what I like to do after a date?"

"Go to the doctor?"

He brought his lips to my ear, "Get naked."

And just like that, I was walking into the office sporting wood, walking behind my Omega and wishing it down. Not that it wasn't a pretty regular state for me now that Cam was under my roof, but I preferred to be semi respectable in public.

Cam was called back quickly, and they had him pee in a cup. They took his blood pressure, and weighed him before sending us into a little dark room with an exam table, a cart of computerized stuff, and a huge wall monitor.

"Just have a seat. No need to take anything off today."

I helped Cam up more to touch him than out of necessity.

"So, this is it. We get to see our beautiful baby." I kissed his cheek. That first night we had been there while the tech looked, but neither of us had been in a frame of mind to process what we were seeing. In so many ways, this was the first time for us.

The tech came in and described what he was going to be doing in detail before having Cam lie down and pull his shirt up and his pants down just enough to expose his entire belly. The tech then covered his middle with gel and placed the wand on him.

Thump thump thump thump.

Our baby's heartbeat echoed in the room.

"If you watch the monitor now, I will start clicking things and labeling them for the doctor. If we are lucky, we will even be able to see the sex of your baby. Are you interested in that?"

Cam and I had discussed this multiple times. And while we were both in agreement that a healthy baby was all we cared about, we disagreed on finding out. Cam wanted to be surprised, and I wanted to know, so we were going to pass. He was the one doing all the work. it was his decision.

"We are going to decline," I said.

An arm smacked me across the chest playfully — or at least I was going to believe playfully. "I'm the patient. I decide." He stuck out his tongue. Playful it was. "Since it is a surprise whenever I find out, I would like to know today if possible."

"You don't have to." The reason he cited was the same exact reason I had given him. This was his pregnancy, and he needed to feel comfortable with his choice.

"But I want to." He took my hand in his.

"So, yes?" The tech looked at us in amusement.

"Yes." We said at the same time.

"Well then, congratulations, dads. You are going to have a little girl joining you shortly."

A girl. We were having a girl.

The rest of the visit was a blur, my mind focused on the little human Cam was growing. Somehow, seeing her, being told she was perfect and on her way made everything that much more real. I was going to be a dad.

We arrived home around dinnertime, and I was still smiling.

"What can I make you?" I asked Cam as he walked in. Sure, his leg was in a boot, but it was so much better than the hobbling he'd needed to do to get by these past months.

"What I really want is a shower. An honest-to-goodness shower." He held his hand out for me. "Help me?"

"If I help you, my mind is going to be on dirtying you up, not making you clean." I bit my bottom lip. It was true. Just the mere thought of him wet and naked had my pants tight.

"Then you can help me shower again."

I was not going to try and argue my way out of that.

We headed to the bedroom where I helped him take off his clothing and his boot. Without it, he wasn't allowed to put any weight on the leg at all. That worked for me just fine. I enjoyed carrying him. It was 5,000 percent caveman, but I couldn't care less. Holding my strong, sexy Omega in my arms like that was everything.

Once in the bathroom, I set him on the toilet and turned the water on before bringing him into the shower and onto the seat I'd bought online for him.

"Did you need anything else?" *Like a blow job?* He was fully erect, and all I could think about was getting him into my mouth. It wasn't the time, though, and I pushed the thought down.

"Come in with me and help me with my harder-to-reach areas."

The man was trying to kill me. I had my clothing off in record time and joined him.

"May I wash your hair?" I was already getting the shampoo. He gave a nod, and I used the hand sprayer to wet his hair before lathering him up.

"You have a hair fetish." he teased before letting a little moan escape.

"Or I know what you like." I grabbed the sprayer and rinsed away the foam.

"Fair enough." He grabbed the body wash. "Do you know what other things I like?" He handed me the bottle after taking what he needed.

"No, what?"

"Watching my Alpha naked under the water. The way the droplets bead up on his chest, the way his cock is pointing at me, telling me exactly how much it wants to be buried inside me, the way his nipples peak, begging for my teeth."

"You are not making getting clean any easier." Not that I wanted him to stop. Had his leg been healed, I had a feeling we'd already be doing plenty of other things in the shower that did not include getting shower fresh. With his leg, that was just all off the table. Even blowing him risked me getting too exuberant and inadvertently leaning against his injury.

"Best get clean quickly, then, so you can help me, and we can get into bed."

He didn't have to tell me twice. I washed off as quickly as I could and then helped Cam. With him, I took my time, enjoying the excuse I had to memorize his body. Every muscle, every freckle, and his expanding middle where he held our beautiful baby girl until she was ready to join the world.

"Ready to towel off and get some rest?" I shut the water off, wrapped a towel around Cam, and scooped him into my arms. "You look very tired."

I carefully carried him into our room and set him on the edge of our bed where I dried him off and helped him get his boot back on.

"This thing is going to limit us," he grumbled.

"Not tonight it won't," I reassured as I eased him back onto the bed so he could lie with his head on the pillow. I opened the drawer and grabbed a bottle of lube.

"How so?" He eyed the lube as I popped the top and coated my fingers with it.

"Because," I slid into bed beside him, bringing my slick fingers down to his entrance and circling it slowly. "It has been too long since I was inside you and, unlike last time, this isn't two men giving into their lust-filled needs."

I slipped a finger inside Cam, and he bucked into me moaning something about more.

"Oh, this is lust filled." He continued to chase my finger until I added a second one, sliding in and out a few times before turning them just right and nailing his prostate.

"It is," I agreed, "but it's also more. I want to take my time with you. Make love to you slowly. Enjoy the feel of me inside you with nothing between us." Shit, if I kept that up, I was going to explode before I even got inside him. I had a feeling this was going to be a case of good intentions. There was no way I was going to be able to hold out for a slow, sensual evening. At least not the first time.

"Please, Alpha, I need to feel you."

At his plea, I drizzled some lube on my hand, and coated my cock before generously slicking his entrance. Just the sight of his hole had my cock twitching. I between his legs, lining up with his hole and slowly sinking in. It was like fucking coming home.

My height allowed me to reach his lips, but barely, his belly cock-blocking my kisses like a boss, but I was determined. One kiss became two, became a thump on my abdomen.

"Looks like she wants you off her turf." Cam chuckled.

I leaned back, my cock leaving him.

"Hell no, Alpha. You can be all *ohh the wonders of creating life* later. Right now, you need to make love to me." Needy Omega. Absolutely freaking perfect.

I slid back inside him, my hand holding me up enough to not smush him. As his hips bucked, so did mine, and we quickly found a rhythm that sent us both toward our release.

Just as I was about to explode with pleasure, I fisted his cock, wanting to bring him to the edge right along with me. Three strokes later, my hand was covered in his cum as I filled him with mine.

I hovered over him, holding myself up on shaking arms. When I could, I slipped out of him carefully. I propped his leg up on a few pillows and headed toward the bathroom to get us a rag for cleanup.

"Smart thinking, Alpha," were the first words he said.

"You mean getting a towel?"

"Not that silly Alpha. Bringing me home that night, the night we made our baby."

I kissed the side of his neck. "As I recall, it was your idea to get out of there." Reaching over, I grabbed the covers and pulled them over us. Getting up was not a thing we were going to be doing. Not until after a small nap, anyway.

"Then, smart thinking, Omega."

I planned to banter back and forth with him, but my body had other ideas, and I fell asleep next to the man who had become my life.

Chapter Twelve

Cam

I was walking on cloud nine. Well, actually I was walking across the street from the fire department to the police station, and I wasn't walking so much as I was limping. The walking boot allowed me to move, but it made one leg about two inches longer than the other, so walking was awkward at best. But it was a thousand times better than the stinky, itchy cast.

It had been two months since I'd broken my leg. I was six months pregnant, but I could still move pretty well, and it was getting better each day. Soon the boot would come off completely and I could get back to working a regular schedule. Not fighting fires, but I could still work for the department. I'd just finished my meeting with the mayor and the fire chief. They'd loved the ideas that I'd put together for the town, and they wanted me to head up the committee that would plan the new events. I'd presented my detailed plans for a summer picnic featuring bouncy houses and games for the kids, a beer tent for the adults, even a speed dating game for the singles in the area. I'd tried to think of everything, and everyone, and since I had a lot of time on my hands to plan, it wasn't that difficult.

I wanted to share the good news with Derek. He was on duty at the moment, and I was having trouble getting hold of him, they were spread pretty thin now that Turner was on paternity leave. Kayden had given birth to their baby girl just last week. She was a cute little thing, based on the pictures they'd sent.

I pulled the door to the police station open and walked in. The place was quiet. Rita sat behind the reception desk, working dispatch.

"Hey, Rita, is Derek around?"

"No. He and Ned went out on a call. They got a lead on that Alpha, Nick Graham, who's after you."

"Oh yeah?" I said, surprised Derek hadn't told me. The trail had gone cold weeks ago. I'd begun to assume he'd given up, though Derek never had. "Credible?"

"Appears to be," she said. "They've been gone about an hour. They haven't called for backup, so that's probably a good sign."

"Well," I said. "I don't have anything better to do. You mind if I hang out a minute? I'll see if I can get hold of Derek."

"Feel free."

I took a seat next to one of the desks. There were only four in the open space, aside from the reception desk. There was a small waiting area, but I chose to sit behind Rita in the bullpen.

I looked over at Derek's office. The light was off, and the shades were drawn so I couldn't see inside. I didn't want to sit in there. It tended to be a little too warm for my liking, and these days I overheated easily.

I pulled out my phone, about to send him a text message when the door opened and my Alpha walked in, looking hotter than ever. I loved the way he looked in his uniform. His walk, his broad shoulders, his chest, everything. I smiled when I saw him, but he didn't smile back. His face drew back in a frown.

"Cam? What are you doing here?"

I tried not to be hurt at his tone of voice, but it was such a change from what I was used to.

"I came by to say hi," I said. "I had that meeting with Harrison and Barry."

"You can't be here right now," he growled. "You need to leave."

"What? Why?" I stood and took a few steps toward him.

He lifted his hand to stop me. I wasn't feeling like being bossed around today, though, and I kept moving.

Ned opened the door and pushed in a man in handcuffs. Ned had one hand on his shoulder, the other on the man's hands, in cuffs behind his back.

I recognized him as my old neighbor, the guy who'd tried to break into Derek's home, Nick Graham. "You've got him," I smiled at Derek. "I knew you would."

"I don't want you here for this," he said. "I don't want him near you."

"He's in handcuffs," I said. "It's fine, but I'll go if you really want."

"Yes," he said. "Please."

Damn Alphas and their Alpha nature.

I grabbed my phone from the desk that I was at, and Ned pushed Nick Graham into the bullpen area. He stood him in front of the desk directly across from me. I met Nick's eyes. They were blazed out, bloodshot, like the man hadn't slept for days, or he was completely blitzed on some mind-altering substance. His eyes were vacant, but then recognition hit.

I heard the click of the keys. Ned took off one handcuff to attach it to the bar on the desk so Nick could sit, but still be restrained. In a split second, fury washed over his face, and Nick was just quick enough to pull away and launch for me.

It happened so fast, I didn't get a chance to move, and I couldn't move that fast even if I'd wanted to. Nick got an arm around my neck, and he hid behind me. He didn't have a weapon in his hand, but his strength took me by surprise. I was at his mercy.

"Well, look what the cop dragged in," he said. "Didn't expect to find you here, Omega. Don't they lock pregnant things like you up in a house somewhere, making sandwiches?"

"Fuck you." I struggled against his hold.

His grip around my neck tightened, and I met Derek's gaze. He was ten steps away, his gun drawn and aimed at Nick.

"Let him go." The authority in Derek's voice unmistakable.

Nick wavered but turned me around so that I was in the direct line of fire. "Don't even think about it, Chief. I'd say this is fair. My Omega for yours. I lost mine. Now, I'm taking yours from you."

"You lost yours to greed, Graham. Let go of him."

I met Derek's gaze from across the room, trying to convey everything I felt at that moment. I loved him. I wanted him to know that. I knew it now. I wish I had told him. Wished we weren't in this situation right then. There was too much I hadn't said, too many things we hadn't discussed yet about our relationship. And why? Because I had been too stubborn? I'd assumed future Cam would figure it all out.

"Don't do anything stupid," Derek said.

I wasn't sure if he was talking to me or to Nick. But, either way, I wasn't going to listen. Nick was a scrawny Alpha, used up from drugs and God knows what else. Sure, he'd lost his Omega, but that was by his own doing. I could feel for him, but only to a point, and I needed to protect myself and my child.

I had been holding on to Nick's arm that was around my neck. I let go of it and brought my elbow down into his midsection as hard as I could. When his arm released from around my neck, I spun around, pivoting on my good leg, and slammed my fist into his face. I put into it as much anger as I could muster. Anger at him for putting me and my family in danger. Anger at myself for not listening to my Alpha.

He flew across the room and slammed against one of the desks then crumpled to the floor.

Derek holstered his weapon and went to him, put handcuffs on him—probably tighter than they needed to be—then left him there.

Derek was at my side, pulling me into his embrace. "Cam, you scared the shit out of me."

"I know," I said. "I'm sorry. I couldn't have his hands on me any longer."

Despite the fact Derek knew I was perfectly fine, having watched the entire interaction, he ran his hands down my back, arms, and torso, rested them gently on my belly. Then he cupped my face and kissed me. The kiss was full of desperation and love.

I moaned against him, wanting to fill my senses with his scent, taste, and touch, wiping away all memory of Nick having his hands on me.

After a moment, Rita cleared her throat. "I've got the state police on their way to pick up this dirt bag," she said. "After that little stunt, he'll be rotting in a jail cell for a while."

"Thanks, Rita," Derek replied, still holding me.

"Do I get to go home now? I'm kind of tired," I said.

Derek hoisted me into his arms.

"What are you doing?" I was not a small Omega, and I had long since given up the dream of having an Alpha that would be willing to pick me up and carry me over the threshold someday, but Derek exceeded all my expectations in every area, including this one. He never stopped picking me up.

"You need to elevate your foot. I want you checked over by a doctor immediately."

"Okay, well, that's not necessary. Not even a little bit. You were here the whole time. He had me in a headlock for all of two minutes."

"Still, you shouldn't be moving on that leg like that."

"Whatever you say, Alpha." I rested against him.

"There," he said. "That's more like it."

Chapter Thirteen

Derek

"I told you I was fine." Cam stuck his tongue out playfully as we left the ER.

As much as he tried to tell me he was fine, and as much as my eyes saw he hadn't been seriously injured, I'd needed to hear from a professional that he and our baby were safe.

"It made me feel better." And that was all there was to say on that.

"You are such an Alpha." Cam rolled his eyes and took my hand. Ever since we finally gave in to the pull between us and made love, he had been expressive like this. A hand hold here, a squeeze on the shoulder there. I was in heaven.

"I'm your Alpha.

"You are." His lips caressed my cheek as we headed out to the car.

We climbed inside, and I turned the ignition.

"Where to, Cam? Want to grab a burger or a Pregnant Omega special?" Going to Bowman's for a meal had become our routine. It was our spot. But, today, what I truly wanted to do was to go home and climb into bed and hold him close. Possibly naked. Definitely naked.

"Can we stop at the bank? My insurance for my place finally came in, and I need to deposit it."

My stomach sank.

"Okay." I pulled out of our parking spot and down the street, terrified of what this might mean. It was unspoken, but the insurance settlement was his way to begin again in a new place—without me.

The bank parking lot had more cars than normal, so when I parked, we were not as close to the entrance as we would have wanted.

"Wait, let me drop you off." Why hadn't I thought of that before? *Because you are scared of losing your Omega.*

"This is fine. Want to come in—what's wrong?" Cam had undone his seatbelt and turned in my direction.

"Nothing. I'm fine. Long day." I undid my seatbelt, ready to walk in with Cam. I knew there was no point in arguing about driving closer to the bank to drop him off.

"Don't. Don't do that. You can tell me anything."

"I don't want you to move out." And I hadn't been man enough to ask him to stay for always.

"Silly Alpha. What makes you think you could get rid of me?"

"You have the money to move now." I shrugged, relief flooding into me. He was staying. I still didn't know what it all meant, but the joy of his words had me floating.

"I had the money to move in my savings all along." Cam's famous eye roll resurfaced. "I wasn't staying for that." He took both my hands in his. "I was staying for you."

"So, you want to stay. To be a family."

"More than anything." He kissed my lips gently before whispering reverently, "I love you."

"And I love you." I kissed him, pouring all my emotions into the kiss. He was staying—with me—to be my family. Our kiss only broke when a car honked behind us.

"Looks like parking is at a premium," I looked back at the honking minivan and gave a half wave. "We best be going in before they blow a gasket."

Cam's blush as he figured out people were watching us was adorable.

The line at the bank was as expected, given the crappy parking, and standing still took its toll on Cam, his leg giving a slight shake. Most people wouldn't have noticed, but most people didn't watch him the way I did.

"Have a seat, and I'll stand in line for you," I offered.

He just looked at me, wide-eyed, before nodding and settling into a chair outside one of the offices. By the time I got to the front, my stomach was growling. He came to join me and made his deposit, promising the teller he would come back and discuss better options for the money later.

"Let's get you some lunch."

Cam rubbed his sexy belly, and suddenly food was the last thing on my mind.

"Takeaway?" I winked, and he broke out in a quiet chuckle as he raked his eyes over my body, stopping in understanding as they reached my tented uniform.

"Or we could have cereal." Cam gave me another of his eye rolls. Fair enough. I deserved it.

We were back home and setting at the table within a half hour. I'd planned on making a few sandwiches for us, but Cam had other ideas.

"I'm not hungry, Alpha." Cam took my hand. "It's been a long day, and I need you."

He didn't have to say what he needed. We both needed to feel each other, to know we were okay both as a couple and as individuals, to be connected.

I scooped him up, carrying him to our bedroom. Cam didn't even pretend to put up a fight, instead snuggling into me.

"My belly," he whined as I sat him down. "It feels huge today and is going to be in the way." He was already stripping, though. "And my leg is not the strongest."

"I see." I pulled my shirt over my head as I toed off my shoes. "So, does that mean you have a plan?"

"Other than for you to make me come?" The glint in his eye had my cock bouncing. What a sexy Omega.

"Yes, other than that." I unzipped my jeans and pushed them down then stepped out of them, completely naked.

"Hmmm, let's see. I could use my hand here," I wrapped my fingers around his cock and gave it a squeeze, just enough to get him going but not enough to give him any relief. "Or I could use my fingers here." Letting go of his erection, my fingers skimmed down his shaft and straight to his entrance, circling his hole, but never attempting to breach it, even as his hips bucked under my caress.

"Needy Omega. I still have not given you your options." I tsked, bringing my face down close enough that my breath reached his need. "I could use my tongue, of course. Lick your shaft, bringing my lips up to taste the offering of precum waiting for me." I licked it off and *mmmed* in delight. "Or I could bring my tongue here and fuck you with it." I licked from his balls, across the sensitive skin and straight to where I knew he wanted me most. "Is that what you wanted, Omega mine?"

"I had been thinking about scooting to the edge of the bed, but your ideas are so much better. I wish we had time for it all."

"We have our entire lives." I breathed on his hole. Rimming was definitely in the forefront of this afternoon's festivities.

"You want me that long?"

"I want you longer, but that is all we have." I lifted my face so he could see the truth and sincerity in my words.

"I love you, Derek."

"And I you, Cam. Now, settle in. You waited far too long to decide, so now I get to pick."

"What did you—"

I gave him his answer—my tongue circling his entrance before giving him what we both wanted.

****

"I was looking for you." Cam hobbled into the kitchen where I was making my best attempt at tacos. He'd mentioned more than once that they were his favorite, and I figured it couldn't be that hard. I'd been wrong. Or at least not smart enough to buy the seasoning packs at the grocery store to make it easy.

"I figured you needed your sleep and our baby needed you to eat, so I would allow you to do one while I got the other ready." I added some more water like the YouTube video directed.

"You made me tacos?" He pressed a kiss at the back of my neck. "You really do love me."

"More than anything." I turned to give him a quick kiss, not wanting to ruin the masterpiece, or at least potentially edible food I had been making.

"And I am going to live here not because my place is gone but because you want me here?"

Screw it. The meat was getting turned off. I had an Omega to reassure.

"Oh, sweet Cam, I didn't bring you here from the hospital because you had nowhere to go. I wanted you here, and not in that blasted bedroom across the hall, but in my bed. This—having you here—has always been about my desire to have a live with you even if that first night I was running on adrenaline and the need to keep you safe." I cupped his cheeks with my hands.

"And I was pregnant."

"Which was the most amazing news I'd ever received in my life, but not the reason. I wish you could look in here." I removed one hand to point to my heart. "To see how completely filled it is by you. You, Cam."

"Hormones." He blinked away the tears forming in his eyes. Tears I was pretty sure were of joy and not sorrow or anger.

"I love you, Cam. I want this home to be our home or, if you want to start anew, we can get our own place together. I want to wake up each morning with you in my arms and have you be the last person I see before I fall asleep each night."

He stiffened under my touch. "I am still a fireman." Was he referring to his schedule, or was it his fear I would make him quit? Had he not seen how proud I was of his place in the station and the amazing work he did?

"Are you ruining my melodramatic ramblings of love?" Cam quirked his eyebrow.

"Of course I want to keep your job unless there comes a time it is no longer your passion. You are the most amazing Omega. Look at all you have accomplished so far in your short life."

"I'm not that young."

"You say to the old man." Now it was my turn to roll my eyes.

"Can we be done with this conversation?" he asked before bringing his lips to my ear. "I'd rather you use those lips to kiss me senseless."

"And then tacos?" I sassed.

"And then tacos."

And kiss him senseless I did.

Epilogue

Cam

I was sitting on the sofa inside the fire station, whipping Bobby's ass in a game of Mario Kart, when the first contraction hit. At least, it was the first time I'd identified a contraction. The back pain had been escalating for the past couple of days, but I thought it was pretty normal.

"Ow." I winced and sat up straighter then doubled over when that hurt too much.

"Ow what?" Bobby didn't even look away from the TV screen.

"I know what that sound is," Philip offered. "I've heard it before."

"What?" I asked, oblivious.

"I'm calling Derek."

"That's not necessary," I protested. "He's finishing up some paperwork. He wanted to get as much done as possible before the baby came."

"Yeah, I think his time might have run out."

I narrowed my eyes; the pain had subsided just as quickly as it had come. "What do you mean?"

"You are in labor, dumbass." Bobby enunciated every word without looking away from the TV.

I'd dropped my controller, but that didn't stop him from continuing the game. He quickly eliminated my lead.

I stood up, stretched my back, and regretted it immediately. "Oh damn," I said. "That hurts. It feels like…"

"A contraction?" Philip's phone was already in his hand.

"Yeah, I didn't anticipate it hurting so much. I have a pretty high pain tolerance. At least I thought I did."

"Well, let us know how that works out for you." He had the phone to his ear. "Derek, you'd better get over here. Your Omega is in labor." He slipped his phone back into his pocket then walked across the floor to look out the window.

"What are you doing?" I asked.

"I just want to watch him run across the street."

I rolled my eyes but joined him to watch because it was pretty funny watching a grown Alpha dash across the street without looking for traffic. The police chief no less.

"I'm going to get Turner to give them a ticket for jaywalking," Philip said.

We both laughed. I regretted laughing, though, because that hurt. I held my stomach.

"Are they supposed to come on this fast?"

Philip shrugged. "I don't know. I'm not an Omega. I just drove to the hospital. Ollie did all the hard work."

Derek burst into the room, eyes wide. "Are you ready?"

"Yeah, I just— Ow. Ow. Ow. That's not a pleasant feeling."

Derek rushed to my side and swept me into his arms. I'd never get over him picking me up like this, though it was getting more and more difficult for him.

He placed me in the car and drove me to the hospital, surprising me with his calm.

I counted the contractions on my watch. They were forty-five seconds apart when we pulled into the parking lot.

"I can walk to the third floor," I said.

"Like hell you are." He already had a wheelchair in his hands. "Get in, sit down."

"That's not necessary," I said and then a pool of warm wetness trickled down my legs. "On second thought, maybe the wheelchair is a good idea."

"You think?"

It didn't take long for the doctor to come in and determine that we were doing this now. There would be no time for waiting, not time for any sort of pain management. Our little girl was arriving soon.

I had a death grip on Derek's hand, and I shouted and pushed and screamed.

"You're doing great." He wiped the sweat off my brow between my bouts of pushing.

I heaved in a breath. "Is she here? Are we done yet?"

"Sorry, Omega. One more push, okay?"

The next contraction came, and I prepared myself for one last hurrah. "Ahhhh!" I swear I felt the bones in Derek's hand break as I bore down.

Then a piercing scream sliced through the air. Our baby girl.

"She's here," Derek said.

He clipped the cord and placed our little girl in my arms. I grinned down at her. She was beautiful, and had a full head of black hair.

"I can't wait to do this again," I said.

"What? You literally said to me while you were in labor, 'Don't ever do this to me again.'"

I chuckled. "Yeah but look how beautiful she is."

After we'd determined that I'd be staying with Derek permanently, we'd converted the room that had been mine into a nursery. Derek had gotten Philip and Turner to help paint, and we'd furnished it with cartoon versions of cats. I'd even found some vinyl decals to stick on the walls. Poor kid was probably going to be tired of cats and kittens before she turned one.

Derek kissed my temple and held me. "She's beautiful," he said. "You did amazing, Omega."

"Thank you." I turned to look at him. "You did pretty well too, Alpha."

"I love you," he said.

"I love you, too."

Anything For Love Sneak Peak

* The following has not been properly edited and may change
Anything For Love follows shortly after Crying Out Loud and features Alpha Mayor Harrison Bowmand and Omega Alexander.

Prologue
Harrison

My cell phone rang just as I was about to get a drink from the bartender. I saw who it was, and I answered it, slipping into a corner booth so I could have a little bit of privacy. The hotel bar wasn't overly packed, and nobody here knew me anyways, so it didn't matter if they overheard.

"Hey, Derek, what's going on?"

"Just wanted to fill you in on some new developments."

"Oh?" I said.

"I know you're away at your conference right now, but I figured you'd want to know the election results."

I was pretty well a shoe-in for Mayor of Millerstown, but yeah, I was curious what the results had been. The last few months of campaigning had been odd to say the least.

When Ian Miller, the Mayor of Millerstown for the past thirty years, kidnapped his grandson because he'd been accused on money laundering, I'd been shocked. Not about the money-laundering, I'd suspected that for years, which is why I'd contacted the FBI about it in the first place. I'd expected a slow-moving investigation, not a shoot-out at the OK Corral.

Since I'd already put in my name for the coming election, the town council had voted me as interim Mayor after Ian was arrested. I'd happily accepted the job. Yesterday had been election day.

"Congratulations, you're the new Mayor of Millerstown."

I grinned, happiness blossoming in my chest. I had so many plans for my hometown and I knew as Mayor I'd help the come to fruition. I couldn't wait to get started. So far as the interim Mayor all I'd done was run clean up on the things Ian Miller had destroyed, including the town morale.

"Thanks man, I wish I could be there to celebrate right now, but this conference…"

"It's all right. It wasn't a surprise anyway."

"I know. Still feels good."

"Yeah. I really look forward to working with you, Harrison. Or should I call you Mr. Mayor?"

I rolled my eyes. Derek was a few years older than me, but we got along pretty well. I couldn't ask for a better Police Chief. "That won't be necessary."

"I wasn't going to do it anyway."

"Thanks for calling, Derek. I appreciate it."

"Anytime."

I hung up the phone and slipped it back into my pocket.

I was going to stay an extra night. But maybe I'll rush home tomorrow so I can be there to get started. I resisted the urge to jump up and pump my fist in the air. I'd been planning to run for town mayor against five term Mayor Ian Miller for years now. The man single handedly ran the town into the ground. He did nothing to engage the citizens and make Millerstown a better place. Whereas I had plenty of plans to do just that. I'd already begun working on them and with the help of a residence we'd already started planning an annual town picnic.

Finally, things were falling in the line. Obviously, there was a lot of work to do.

Since I had only one night in the city away from the prying eyes of Millerstown citizens, I might as well enjoy myself. Maybe pick up something sweet to take back to my hotel room and enjoy.

I went back to the bar. Where I had been sitting there was now a gorgeous Omega standing there. He rested his elbows on the bar and was talking animatedly to the bartender. His face was lit with excitement as he spoke. The bartender rushed off to the side to take care of another customer and so I swooped in.

"Hello, handsome, can I get you something?" Admittedly, not my best opening line, but I was completely out of practice.

The young man turned to look at me, his blue eyes shining in the dim light of the bar. He looked surprised for a minute, then looked around. "Me?" he asked.

I grinned. "Yeah you." I narrowed my eyes. "You look a little bit familiar. What's your name?" I asked.

"Umm. Lex. Alexander," the Omega answered.

"I'm Harry. It's nice to meet you." I reached out a hand and he shook it.

"Nice to meet you, too."

"Listen," I said. "I'm only in town for the night and I just got some really good news and I'd like to celebrate."

"Oh," he said with a raise brow. "What sort of news?" A grin tugged at the corner of his lips.

"I got a job that I'd been trying to get for a while now. So, I just want to celebrate. Would you be interested in celebrating with me?"

The Omega bit his lip. He looked around to the bartender, then back to me. "Um. Sure," he said. "I'm going to tell my cousin where I'm going though. Where am I going?"

"It's right upstairs. Room four thirty-five."

"All right." He went to the corner of the bar told his cousin or so he claimed, where he was going and then came back to me. "Lead the way," he said with a smile.

Damn. I hadn't expected it to be so easy. And just for a moment, I thought maybe it had been too easy. What was I thinking? Inviting a stranger to my hotel room? But then he slipped his hand into mine and sparks flew. It was cliché, and I wouldn't have believed it if I hadn't been there, but we had a connection, a spark, that was immediate and overpowering.

We wasted no time when we got to my hotel room. I pushed open the door, tossed my key card and wallet on to side table, when I turned to face Lex, he pounced. His lips crashed on mine and I wrapped my arms around his waist. I hoisted him into the air and walked to the bed.

I tossed him onto the bed and he shot me a sexy grin.

"I really like the way you celebrate," he said.

"Me too." I unbuttoned my shirt, tossed it to the corner of the room when I finally got it off my shoulders.

He pulled his t-shirt over his head and unbuckled his pants. I followed suite and soon the two of use were naked. I took a minute to lazily rake my gaze up and down his gorgeous, lithe body. There was something familiar about his hands, and the angular set to his jaw. I couldn't quite place it.

"What are you waiting for Harry?"

"Nothing, Lex, nothing at all."

I grabbed the lube from my suitcase and slathered some on my fingers, throwing the bottle and a condom on the bed for later use.

I settled between his open legs. His cock already hard for me, just as mine was for him. I opened my mouth and swallowed his dick. Pre-cum splashed on my tongue and I hummed. His hips bucked, so I held them down.

My fingers went to his entrance, pressing gently until his body opened for me.

His hands went to my head and he tugged at my hair, I popped off his cock and looked at him. His eyes were hungry, desire simmering below the surface. I couldn't wait to get in side him.

I ripped open the condom and slipped it on, then lined up to his hole. All the while, Lex watched me.

I pushed in, filling him completely, his body opening as if it was made for me.

He moaned in please and arched his back. "More, Harry, more."

I complied, pounding into him with abandon. His legs opened wider and our skin slapped together with each thrust.

He pumped his dick, matching my rhythm.

"Fuck, that's sexy," I said.

He grinned up at me and pulled me down for a kiss. As our lips met, his cock erupted, spurting cum onto our stomachs.

His body clenched around me, milking my own release to follow soon after his.

As my hips slowed, I kissed his lips again, then trailed kisses across his cheek and down his neck. I breathed in the sweet scent of him. This amazing Omega, who'd given me the best celebration. I wanted more of him.

I slid out of him and fell to his side, pulling him against me. I should get up, should clean us up like a good Alpha would do. And I would. But first, I needed a minute. Needed to hold him against me as we both came down from our orgasmic high.

"Thank you, Harry," he said.

"Mmm hmm," I murmured against his cheek, nuzzling into him. My eyes fluttered closed as I lost my battle to stay awake.

The next morning, I awoke alone. My mystery Omega was gone, leaving me with a lasting memory and a single name, Lex.

Mpreg Titles by Jena Wade

Millerstown Moments

Dashboard Lights (https://www.amazon.com/gp/product/B07MHFQQ3F)
All Revved Up (https://www.amazon.com/dp/B07N16DR5G)
Crying Out Loud (with Lorelei M. Hart) (https://www.amazon.com/gp/product/B07NKXJPRM)
Anything For Love
Life is a Lemon (with Lorelei M. Hart)

Vale Valley Valentine Romance

Picture Purrfect (https://www.amazon.com/dp/B07MM2TP6T)

Dragons Series

Dragon's Fire (http://www.amazon.com/dp/B07GGVSV11)
Dragon's Ice (https://www.amazon.com/dp/B07H73CT81)
Dragon's Stone (https://www.amazon.com/dp/B07HQCVV6S)
Dragon's Jewel (https://www.amazon.com/dp/B07K4YBQ7R)
Dragon's Spark (https://www.amazon.com/dp/B07KW2XNLG)

Directions Series

Up to Code (https://www.amazon.com/dp/B07DBL3W83)
Down to Earth (https://www.amazon.com/dp/B07DZB2PXK)
Back to You (https://www.amazon.com/dp/B07FXNV5MS)

Shorts

Alpha Student (https://www.amazon.com/dp/B07D7GGXZF)
Alpha Doctor (https://mailchi.mp/9b658a089de7/signup)

Jena Wade

Jena lives in Michigan with her husband, two dogs, and three children. By day she works as a web developer and at night she writes. She was born and raised on a farm and spends most of her free time outdoors, playing in the garden or tending to her landscaping.
Find out more about the author at http://www.thejenawade.com/.
Follow Jena on Facebook (https://www.facebook.com/jena.wade.7528) or Twitter (https://twitter.com/thejenawade).

Subscribe to Jena's Newsletter (https://mailchi.mp/9b658a089de7/signup)(she promises not to spam).

Printed in Great Britain
by Amazon